THE VIRTUAL LOVER

THE VIRTUAL LOVER

Vishnu Datt (VDV)

GenNext Publication

ISBN : 978-93-8022-261-5

Price : ₹ 280

First Published, 2015

Published by,

genNext Publication
23, Main Ansari Road, Darya Ganj
New Delhi-110002
Ph. : 23242060, 23261060
Fax : 011-23285914
E-mail: gennext@hotmail.com
Website : www.gyanbooks.com

Laser Typesetting : Rajender Vashist, Delhi.
Printed at : G. Print Process, Delhi.

Cataloging in Publication Data—DK
Courtesy: D.K. Agencies (P) Ltd. <docinfo@dkagencies.com>

Datt, Vishnu.
The virtual lover / Vishnu Datt.
p. cm.
Novel.
ISBN 9789380222615

1. Love stories, Indic (English). I. Title.

DDC 823.92 23

Dedication

Dedicated to my Father Mr O.D. Vashishtha, Mother Mrs Raj Bala; Sisters Bharti and Anamika, my English teacher Sh. Hawa Singh and the Angel behind this novel.

And above all to Him, to the Almighty, who does it all!

So, Prayers to Him!

Prologue

To re-experience the greatest and the most thrilling feeling on the earth–love;

To understand why everyone is special!

To the people who Love someone selflessly;

To jump into joy of doing for someone unknown;

To cherish those wonderful moments of life, begone and brought back to the soul;

To the patience which helps accomplish any task in Life;

To remove the freaking feeling of Loneliness;

To assume the meaning of the word, 'Friend'!

Contents

Acknowledgements

A great start always leads to a brilliant end! Therefore, I would like to start at a creation with the blessings of the Almighty and pay my tribute to the greatest man ever admired by me in my life—My Grandfather, Late Sh. Sube Singh Sharma! May his soul rest in peace and feel proud!

'Thanks' though diminishes the sacrifices of a person for something he/she did for us but it's necessary to tell others about their contributions and motivations.

Thanks to all my teachers and my friends—Manjeet Solanki, Nitish Bhardwaj, Gaurav Kumar Raheja, Sumer Singh, Sahil Bansal, Ajay Godara, Rohit Sharma, Kapil Duhoon and everyone close to me !

A Special Thanks to my brothers Rahul and Rohit, to Uncle Sh. Pawan and Aunt Smt. Indira, and Shivani *Didi* for their moral support!

A very special thanks to all my critics, whose criticism makes me stronger!

Vishnu Datt

1

THE CRUSH

Goddess Saraswati School, Sonepat

An ordinary Mamma-boy was enjoying the cultural activities held in the Activity Hall of the school, in his own way, imagining himself of being the performer (typical daydreamer!). The beats of the music were moving through his heart, as electricity moves through copper wires. He was enjoying every moment of the activities as live, as it could be. Thinking of every step of dance, done by him and every higher and lower notes of the song being played, sung by him.

Suddenly, the touch of his friend Sumer's hand on his knees shattered his dreams, as if he was asking for some kind of help. He was a bit upset as he was dream-feeling himself to be a rock star, and had been brought back to an ordinary schoolboy! As if, a plane landed at an unknown and unsophisticated airport in emergency! Vivek asked him about the reason for bringing him back to the ground. Vivek was in just another world of his dreams and was enjoying like anything.

He replied—"Brother! Please help".

Vivek was a bit worried now when he looked at his friend's pitiful face forgetting about his own dreams. He was more concerned for Sumer, who told him that a girl was using his left knee as a support. They had been sitting there for last one hour. Everyone was getting tired as the time passed by, except Vivek, he was busy at a different platform! Everybody was taking each other's support! Vivek was a bit angry as his enjoyment was disturbed due to Sumer's problem. So he angrily asked Sumer to suggest the girl to take her Knee off his left knee.

"No! I can't".

"Ok! Then let me do this for you, she is a girl only, not a missile."

He pushed Sumer back to shout at her. But not a single word, he could speak. He stopped and moved himself back hiding himself behind Sumer. He looked into other direction, pressing his lips and raising his eyebrows in big surprise. He shook his neck a bit and closed his eyes silently saying, "Oh My God! She is something amazing, so beautiful". After that he kept staring at her only. He was feeling as if he was in heaven and a fairy (as told by his mother in Fairy tale when he was a small child) was before him! He felt embarrassed as he found himself gone a sort of mad, as he was going to speak harshly to this wonderful creation of the Almighty! He now understood, why Sumer hesitated.

He forgot about Sumer's problem and about the dreams, he was enjoying of being a rockstar! Stunned was he, thinking about where she was earlier?

"Is she from the same school where I study? In which standard is she?"

The only thing he could remember was she and he was in the heaven again... He used to see these kind of scenes in Bollywood films but could not stop himself from being a part of those repeated scenes at that time! As if, it was an inexplicable experience for him!

He thanked Sumer for his role in those moments. For the whole day, he was moving through his own thoughts, though physically present in the school. He was mentally lost in his own dreams and those wonderful thoughts! As if all the natural powers were with him—the climate, winds blowing through his silky hair, trees and the human beings around! All were with him in his unreasonable happiness ! Her beautiful face was moving through his thoughts, and thoughts around his eyes, open or closed! He was feeling so fortunate that he saw such a beauty, that day. Thanking God for His wonderful creation! There were no classes that day (as examinations were just over). He was in the tenth standard, the senior most class of the school; his classmates used to enjoy the little mentorship over juniors.

That day was the day first in heaven for him, a good start! The whole day he was thinking about that moment, when he had seen her and her stunningly beautiful face and its radiant features! Those wonderful eyes claimed their appearance anywhere. He did not even go to the playground that evening (something unusual for a sports freak). He had a little dinner that night and went straight to his bedroom. Lying in bed, he asked Goddess Laxmi if she was her counterpart. He did not know when his sleep embraced his thinking about her...!

The next day, he got up early, took bath and was pushing his mother to prepare the breakfast as fast as she could, and told a lie that "From today my Morning extra-classes will be there!"

He was overexcited to see her again, and out of this excitement, he told a lie to his mother! She helped him faster go from the house to school, but when he came out of the house, it was unbelievable for him. She was moving in front of his eyes, riding on a lady-bicycle, on the way that led to their school. He was moving with the same pace afoot behind! It was around 7:25 am and the school started at eight am sharp! That day he saw 'the power of wishes'. If you like someone wholeheartedly, then the whole surroundings around you stand with you, help you the best way. In fact, it is God with you.

She went to the bicycle stand to park her bicycle. He threw his bag in his classroom and saw that she went under the corridor somewhere on the groundfloor. He could not follow her further, as she had gone beyond his sight. He wanted to chase her to know about the class she studied in as well as to confirm the time she came to the school. As he lost her from sight the corridor onwards, he moved straight up to the top floor, to see from there, if she was visible somewhere. As he was looking down, she appeared from the left hand side stairs. She looked at him, for less than a moment and went straight to her classroom. He kept standing there, stunned. He came to know that she was in his younger sister Ana's class, in the eighth standard and she came so early because their Extra-classes started in the morning 7:30. He was never in the school before 7:50. He realised that the lie he told his mother was under God's purpose of helping him know more about her. He then went to his classroom. The students who used to come earlier to him from far away villages in the early morning due to the bus timings, were surprised to see him at 7:35 in school. They were asking him for the reason which couldn't be shared with them, so he replied—"Well, nothing special, I got up a bit early today as I have started working up for a strong build—go for running and exercises for that. All this is just to maintain my body, you know". He gave the reasons in advance to stop his class-fellows from asking anything further.

Now, he got ample of time to think of the ways to ask his younger sister about her classmate–her name, nature and everything. He thought about it till lunchtime, and as soon as the bell was beaten, he moved to his sister's class with his tiffin. It was so unusual for his sister. She got surprised to see him there and that too for the lunch! She had queries in her mind but still was happy and proud to see her brother there for the first time during the lunchtime, when they were in the same school for last ten years. He never came to her once in these ten years. That day, his surprising entry compelled his younger sister to raise her eyebrows, with many questions in her mind.

He was having lunch with his sister apparently feeling her presence, too. She was sitting behind them. The lunch was awesome for Vivek. He then came to his classroom without asking anything from his sister about her. He left her in a great surprise for why in so many years of studying together, he had lunch with her for the first time that day!

Again, at the end of the school hour at two, he was waiting to get a glance of that beauty. He stood at the doors of his classroom and there came the breathtaking moment for him, when the girl of the bright face and small hairs was in front of his eyes. His breath stopped for some moments. He went home happily and then stood on the roof of his house, to see her going on the same bicycle. He cherished the moment when she passed by him, way back to her house.

It was evening when his sister Ana asked him the reason behind his going to her classroom? He thought for a while and said—

"Nothing sis! Just to share lunch with you today."

She was not satisfied and asked their elder sister Drishti to ask him for the reason behind his visit to her class. Now, he had to be strong enough to say the same words again but his elder sister was satisfied with his answer, so he escaped. Similar days passed by and he used to follow the same schedule everyday. The first look of her, used to make his whole day interesting in the school and he used to feel great at heart that she was together in the same building for hours!

One day, he much bravely asked his younger sister Ana about her indirectly, telling her a lie and asking for a favour. He said to her—"My best friend Manjeet likes her and has challenged me, that, if I can talk to her or get her name known, he will give me a Navy Watch." Seeing the challenge to be very simple and taking it for granted, Ana told him that her name was 'LAXMI' and she is a very tough girl to talk to...! He was so happy to know her name and gave himself a pat on the shoulder for his intelligence in finding out her name.

Two days later, a notice charmed him announcing a school trip to Appu Ghar; a water park in New Delhi. Vivek got much excited about it. He asked his sister if she was going to Appu Ghar? She said—"Yes!"

Then, he asked her about Laxmi on behalf of Manjeet.

"She is not going as her best friend Aarti is not going".

"And why Aarti is not going?"

"Well, I think her parents did not allow. But why are you so interested?", asked a doubtful Ana.

Whole of his excitement came to level zero with this question.

"Chh...I told you–for Manjeet. What did you think?" answered Vivek, escaping her doubts.

He paid for the trip unhappily but with a wish in his heart, that Laxmi might accompany as well. All the participants who submitted the money had to gather at the assembly hall that day at 1:30 pm sharp. He went to the gathering with a wish in his heart that she and her best friend would go to Appu Ghar as well. He was again, filled with joy when he saw his sister, Laxmi and her friend Aarti there. He could not express the happiness, he was enjoying alone that time, thanking God for His magic. His wish had come true. The next day they had to visit Appu Ghar. But before that, they gathered at the school reception at 6:30 am sharp.

Visit to Appu Ghar

The next day Vivek and Ana went to school at right time and boarded the buses with some chips and biscuits. He could see her sitting in the other bus and felt happy again to confirm her visit, shaking his head with a childish smile. While boys were shouting to see the boy's bus overtake the girl's, he was busy trying to catch a glimpse of Laxmi. He was listening to the songs, being played in the bus, imagining Laxmi in mind and enjoying the journey. They reached Appu Ghar at 8:00 am sharp and had to stand there in a queue for the ticket. He was searching for her, as there was a separate line for girls. He looked at every single face, but couldn't find her. As soon as, he turned his face to the other side in disappointment, there she was laughing with her friend Aarti. A thirsty crow got his water.

They entered the water park. All the students were divided into different groups to enjoy in a disciplined manner. Girls and boys were separated, as some boys were notorious and abusive in nature. This was sad for him, still he tried to console himself. Now, half-heartedly, Vivek was enjoying the different slides of the water park with his friends.

Meanwhile many funny incidents happened. Their science teacher was so eager to ride the water slide but was not sure if he could do that, he came down the slide in a sitting position holding the boundaries of the slide out of fear. Manjeet did not know swimming and the way he was trying! Kavinder's underwear coming down, when he was jumping from water and many such events. He had to wait for an hour to get a glimpse of her. He was taking every dip in the water with a prayerful thought that he might see her, when he comes out. With a deep breath, he took a dip inside water and said to God, 'I will not come out, unless you show me her glimpse'. He came out on the water, when he could not hold his breath any longer, tried to find her, but could not, so taking another deep breath, he went deeper through the water. It was becoming difficult for him to hold his breath under water, so he came out again and again. His friends asked him in a concerned tone, "Hey! What are you doing? Are you trying to die?"

To this, he replied while his eyes were busy searching for her, "You do your work, I am doing mine". God does not take much time to fulfill the wishes of a clean heart. In the third attempt, as he came out, the reflected sunrays entered his eyes and compelled them to blink. When he tried to concentrate, he saw the water droplets on the face. It was she, enjoying another water slide in front of his eyes, very excited and happy! She was wearing a red top with blue lower and her complexion shone brighter in that wet dress! He was praying to God — "O Lord! May she keep standing in front of me and I get a chance to see her young bud-beauty more clearly to purify my soul to the core!"

They all had a wonderful lunch there and again in a queue they moved towards the different swings at the Appu Ghar. The swings were moving taking both of them, in itself as if, they were the hands of time machine and he was looking at her as if she was his! All the rides in the Appu Ghar were worth remembering for the whole life of Vivek! He was trying hard to ride on the same swing she was on, though his sister Ana was keeping a closer look at his activities at that time. Every time, she was saying— "*Tu ghar chal beta, Didi ko bataungi*" and to this he replied— "What? I have to take care of you here, you know that!"

You can never stop a lover like that, as he gets notorious with restrictions.

The climate in the evening got amazing, as if God was scattering his love over all of them, the setting sun, clouds and all. In the end, they all had to gather at the main entrance of Appu Ghar to see that none was left out there from the lot. The teachers gave Vivek the duty to make a line of a group of students. He took the lead and ordered holding the arms of the first child in line, "Be in a line", the authority in his voice was clear. As he looked at the first child he was holding the shoulders in his hands, he lost the control of his nerves, for he understood and his hands responded accordingly, leaving the grip slowly! It was she–his beloved! It was a lifetime experience and, her first and last touch he could feel. When he realised it, he saw at her face and as usual, she did not look even once at Vivek and her shyness again compelled him to fall in love with her deep beauty.

They boarded the buses back to Sonipat. He was still feeling her touch in his hands. Every moment of this journey was so thrilling for him, with her thoughts in his mind, with every movement of her those beautiful eyes, with her wonderful smiles. Those sinful killing looks and that fairylike beauty was killing him every moment he was remembering her. They reached back to the school at 8:30 pm at night and he went to his sister's class to take her along and get a last glimpse of Laxmi for that night. He wished her a good bye from heart and moved home with his sister Ana. Each moment of that wonderful trip to Appu Ghar was very special for him for the rest of his life. Though the Appu Ghar has been replaced with a metro station named Pragati Maidan. However, whenever he went by that place, his memories welled up afresh.

Normal School Life and Board Examination

After the trip, the normal school life started for Vivek. Only a few days were left in the school for them as board examinations were approaching near. He was counting the days left, always looking at her and thinking that only after a few days, he would not see her ever again. He thought her to be his always and for this, he exercised a lot to gain a better frame of his body as he came to know that her father was in police. He used to think that no power in this world could stop him from befriending her. None would stop the accomplishment of his wish! He was stronger but felt least before her. He could not ask her once for her autographs in the slam book, even after trying several times. He went back home sadly. Otherwise, he was becoming stronger day by day and his daily diet began to surprise his father as he once expressed– "Ten *chapattis* at one time, are you man or animal?"

He never studied as does a normal sent-up board student more than twelve hours a day and his mother used to goad– "Son, study something, otherwise you will fail in Boards!"

He thought that God was with him. So, whatever he studied, helped him. He took all his Board examinations and every paper seemed to be very easy, as after each paper he assured his father to obtain more than 90 per cent. Time glided as life was going to take a U-turn for Vivek. Many days had passed. He had not seen her once. He was living only with the cherishing memories of her with him. During the holidays after the Board examination, he visited the school to butter the peon, so that he could see the class registers and the old photographs of the school functions. He used his mind again to know her permanent address through her class register and thanked God again for the same.

Admission in Eleventh Class

He got admission for eleventh standard in a new school, situated on the same way, which Laxmi used to travel daily to her old school. His new school, Hind Shikshapeeth, was near her house. He used to see her daily and again his school time used to be enjoyable! He went to school for a month only for the long summer vacation were approaching for the months of June-July. He gave his seasonal tests and the holidays started! Everybody was so happy but him, as in these holidays he would not get a chance to see her! He became imaginative and wrote few lines for his feelings—

All are happy and I am sad,
As something happened bad,
It is my time to bear,
Nobody close to hear,
Let me handle, with a candle,
As I am not a part of scandal,
I will fight and I will try to overcome,
I can speak but have to be dumb,
He (God) is there who will decide,
That's why my sorrows, I have to hide!

2

THE DISTANCE

Summer Holidays

The summer holidays began with an uninteresting start for Vivek. All his friends used to gather in the playground daily-morning and evening. In his new school, the admissions took place on the basis of Board Examination results, that had to be declared during the holidays. It was on 23rd of May, 2005 when his younger sister Ana asked him to do her a favour at around four in evening. That time he was getting ready to go to the play fields. He asked her—"What do you want to buy?"

"Some clay. Any idea, where we can find it in Sonipat?" asked Ana.

A lover's mind is always sensitive. He immediately corelated of going to the market, that was near Laxmi's house and said—"Yes, I know. But the shop is a bit far away. Would you like to go there with me on bicycle?"

"Yes, anything for it. I need it in any case", replied Ana, in need.

They went to the market near Laxmi's house and he

then asked his sister to go and ask at every shop there for clay. As she was busy asking for clay in different shops, he was standing outside in hope and thinking-"I wish, she comes here and I would then be lucky to see her in her casual dress as well".

"There is nothing available here like clay. All the shopkeepers are asking me—'Who told you that you will find clay here?' You weird boy! you are standing outside yourself asking me to face these shopkeepers? Why did you come here, if you can't help me? I can smell something cooking in your mind again".

They came back bare-handed as they could not find anything else than a limestone, among the many things, they had gone to buy. For the whole time they were near Laxmi's house, Vivek expected about various scenes, like he would just look into the direction of her house and she would be with her mother and a bag in her hand, shopping around, and many other thoughts were hovering his mind. However, nothing happened actually. As they came back, the first sentence he heard shockingly was—"VU, your result has come. You have obtained 80 per cent marks in your Boards!"

His sister told him about it when he was opening the main door of their house and parking his bicycle.

His high dreams suddenly shattered with these words of his sister. He now knew that he would not be eligible to get admission in the same school, he was thinking of. He tried his level best to satisfy himself with the unwanted result. His father perturbed after hearing about his results told his mother about the results of the children there in Chandigarh. However still, the next day he prayed to God and tried the last time to go to the same school and get admission there. As he reached the school gate on bicycle after finishing some work in the way, his mother called from behind loudly, asking him to stop, and told him— "You need not try for admission here, as your father has arranged for your admission in Chandigarh."

This was shocking for Vivek. However, he soon made up his mind completely for Chandigarh. He sensed meanwhile loss of dedication to freinds on his part and had himself to remove such shortcoming in all promptness. That day in the evening, he went to meet all his friends at the playground to convey them about his departure. They all grew sad.

"Which city is better in terms of education—Sonepat or Chandigarh?" was much discussed among them.

He bade them a final bye and moved back promising that he would keep coming regularly to meet them. That night, he had a big task to do as his father announced of the departure to Chandigarh next day. The task of collecting all the important stuff required there for their common needs and collecting the memories of his beloved's birthplace, which was quite difficult as his whole life was full of this place only. He was leaving behind—the streets, the school, the family, the friends, the playground, and above all the land itself! He was remembering the whole life; he spent there. He kept his personal diary, the autograph book, and some books which could help him in the eleventh standard. The next morning, they started the journey, which was taking just everything from him, as they were moving forward to Chandigarh.

Chandigarh Life

They reached Chandigarh bus stand around two pm where his father had come to pick them. They reached their new home in Panchkula, which was a beautiful place with a garden in the front, flowers, trees...nature and a lift in the building. It was enough to attract a person, who lived at a place without gardens; symmetrical trees planted everywhere, curtains in the house, a three bedroom set apartment with two sided lobbies, clean roads, smart people around and everything out there.

Panchkula was the first planned city of Haryana according to his knowledge and a part of tricity—Chandigarh, Mohali and Panchkula. He wrote a few lines here about the mother earth influenced by the gardener's creativity—

A place to live for human being,
Where the nature can sing,
With birds chirping, winds blowing,
All happy and soothing,
No sorrow, but happiness around,
The mountains, rivers and the ground,
A way with green trees and flowers laid,
God! How happy an Earth you have made!

He found this new place full of dense trees planted either side of roads, big parks where people could walk, exercise and enjoy nature in their own way and could meet each other. That very first night in Panchkula was a night worth remembering for him as he was asking questions to the Almighty and himself—

"Where have I come, and what is all going on? Do I have to live here now onwards and forget my birthplace forever? Is it not possible that my birthplace become as planned as this place? What would happen, when I will go to my new school situated at Chandigarh for the first time?"

The next day they started from Panchkula to Chandigarh in the same old car they called 'Dear Grandmother-Maruti 800' for admission purpose. They reached the school in time but due to his habit of regular silly mistakes, he forgot to take his passport size photographs, which were necessary for the admission procedure in the school. After some regular angry words to him, his father took him to the nearby market in the same Sector-7 and got his emergency photographs—snapped and returned to the school. After waiting for a while, a teacher came asking them about their arrival at school. His father had a little chat with her and she just came to Vivek and asked him a few questions to which he replied confidently, though surprisingly, because one question was from Chemistry, he studied in his old school. He replied pretty quickly—

"Atomic structure!"

He actually did not know anything about it at that time. Therefore, he was amazed about how he replied so quickly. Most probably, it was Goddess Saraswati's blessings on him that day. His future was destined there for the next two years for sure. Sometimes the things are not in your hands, and sometimes they are not even in others' hands, too. Like his admission in Kailash Public School. But one thing he was thinking about was—

"The chemistry teacher was the only person ever to say that 80 per cent marks in Boards was a great score!"

He got admission to the school with some formalities and submission of important papers, like score cards and character certificate. He was asked by the teacher if he would attend the classes the same day or from the next day, to which he was about to answer a "NO", but before he could say anything, his father said—

"Of course, Ma'm! Why not from today?"

He looked with a surprise, towards his father and mumed unlistened—

"Don't you like me? If yes, then why are you handing me over to these unknown people!"

However, neither did he ask him nor he would have answered in his expected way. He was not wearing a formal school uniform, not because he did not have one that day instead because he was mentally prepared not to attend the school the very first day.

He felt embarrassed that whole day as every teacher identified him easily and asked questions about his late admission. He was afraid of asking anyone about what was going on, and was answering the questions in a stupid manner, as he was untouched of the studies from last so many days. The peon told him to sit in the school bus No. 3 for Panchkula, which he found easily. He was quite unknown about the routes and the identical sectors in both Panchkula and Chandigarh and the confusing roundabout after each sector! The bus driver stopped the bus before their apartments and asked him— "Brother, which sector?"

"Fourteen!"

"Which place in sector fourteen ?"

"Near petrol pump".

"Then, get down here only, it's nearby!"

He got down and started moving in a direction, which was taking him to the petrol pump but away from his residence. Suddenly, the gatekeeper of their apartment recognised him and called from behind—

"Sir, where are you going? Your house is here, where are you going?"

"Nowhere, I was coming here only". He wisely concealed his mistake.

The same evening his father came early from the office and took him to the same place where his school was situated and asked him about the day, one of his usual questions. He shared his experience, the real one, that Sonipat schools were better. To which his father disagreed. They bought a new school uniform, some books and copies, which were costlier than they were thinking of, and came back home.

The first day was over.

It was Friday and two successive holidays—Saturday

and Sunday—were coming, as told to him by a classmate. He was told by his father that he will have to ask some classmate about the tuition classes, something unusual for him again, on Monday.

He fortunately got the bus on Monday morning and got a chance to talk to the bus driver for further assistance and finalise the 'pick and drop' place for him. He talked to Rosh for the first time in his new school and asked him some questions, though Rosh was not interested in answering any one. However, Vivek had to know through the question in any case. He thought the students were not much friendly there and there was also a dialect problem. Therefore, he used to keep quiet in the class most of the time and observed the way they spoke and interacted. He had to forget his *Haryanvi* tone to interact with them and share ideas or views. Occasionally, he used to speak in *Haryanvi* with his only friend, Vikram, who was from Najafgarh, Delhi. He was learning a new way of expressing oneself and Hindi was emerging like a great language, for him. However, it was a bit difficult but he managed somehow.

For last few days, he was normal like typical nature of Indians to adjust in any kind of atmosphere. His daily life was almost the same—waking up, getting ready, catching school bus, school time, back home, taking some rest, taking tuitions, coming back, studying after dinner and sweet dreams. Nothing special was going on except he was becoming poorer in studies, making his father more concerned about his future and studies. Nevertheless, Vivek always used to think positively—

"I will get whatever I am here for".

However, this nature of Vivek seemed to his father a typically casual behaviour towards studies and life!

It seemed to him as if some unknown force was not allowing him to succeed at that time even after his hard work. He used to enjoy his whole day with a friend, who was going through the same experiences as himself—Gaurav Raheja. He was the person from whom, he could know about the word—TRUST. He was the person whom you could trust with closed eyes— "A God's Gift!" He knew about Vivek's daily routine, which they both used to follow.

His eleventh standard concluded in random experiencing the new environment and harsh studies to which he got somewhat allergic those days. He and Gaurav just managed to pass that year. They were 'pushed' to twelfth standard on conditions that they had to show good results in future. Vivek was trying the whole time to buck up in all subjects, and specially in computers, which was never a subject of interest for him. It was not that he did not try to learn it, but what else he could do, when even after trying so much in the whole eleventh standard, he was not able to write even a single and the simplest programme. 'Errors' were the only visuals he was able to find on the computer screen. He used to get surprised always to see his classmates running their individual programmes correctly. He copied the programme but to find some inevitable errors. He grew so nervous to take his *viva-voice* for the subject, that too at the end. The teacher very sweetly asked him— "Do you know the sign of input-output operators?"

He was so happy and wrote the signs of the operators on his sheet right away. The teacher then asked— "Which one of this is the Input operator? Just tell me and I will give you enough marks to pass at least!"

Moreover, what else one could expect from him? He replied to it wrongly. What else could the teacher say then...?

"Please change your additional subject, if possible!"

The beginning of twelfth standard was a bit boosting for

him as he got 50 per cent and above in the first term examinations, but the only problem was his weakness in the computer subject. Gaurav had taken physical education as an additional subject, which was much easier than computers. Vivek, too, convinced so far was interested in taking physical education and so requested his father to let him change his additional subject. He knew that his father wanted to make him a perfect child and in this fast moving modern world, wanted him to learn computers as much as he could, the latest trend. He always kept on telling him to remain updated with all the happenings around. Therefore, he had to do a lot of dramatic stuff before him to get the answer as—“YES!” He got his additional subject changed and used to enjoy its period daily as they used to play volleyball and ‘with God’s grace’ he used to hit hard goals. The power, he was blessed with from his birthplace, was still inside. In the class, there used to be a consistant sitting plan, according to which they both, Gaurav and Vivek, used to sit just behind the two most ‘beauty-fuel’ girls Vishakha and Youvi. He called them his sisters and they helped him and Gaurav know more about that place and the people. Vivek called them ‘beauty-fuel’ because they were so charming and helping that whenever he and Gaurav used to be sad, they always helped them getting out of that tension and lightened up the atmosphere with their helping nature and charm. They both also teased him, as his sisters did at home. He used to enjoy during the school time, for after that he was there to perform the most unwanted thing—studies!

Vivek and Gaurav were famous for two things in the whole class—first, they were poor in studies, and second, they were good in humour. In the early days of twelfth standard, some guys and girls of their class and the school management decided to organise a freshers’ party for the newly admitted twelfth standard students. They (Gaurav and Vivek) did not know at first about that, however, they were excited to join it, as typical entertainment seekers.

They enjoyed the freshers' party very much, as some funny incidents were a part of it. For instance, their mathematics teacher danced on their request but in a quite strange and funny way; Gaurav danced for the first time ever as he told them, but it was a good show from him. In addition, the last but not the least, a group of girls asked Vivek to come and dance with them as they were attracted towards his dancing skills. But it was difficult for him to say—"Yes!" He was a person who did not even talk to any girl, how could he dance with a group? However, in the end he performed well to raise many wonder-eyebrows. The freshers' party was a real fun for them, and when he reached home, he realised that his shirt was really wet, like a shirt taken out of the washing machine without drying. He had danced that day to limits. After that day, no more entertainment happened for Vivek, as the serious time had started with reverse gear to the daily drama—same schedule to follow and the same life to live.

The Chemistry Paper

The schedule was so hectic and busy, that one day, it happened to be a shocking day for Vivek. He boarded his school bus at the normal time and the journey started to the school. Their pre-board examinations were going on and he was studying his chemistry book while riding in the bus. A very few students were present in the bus. The examinations were on different dates and everyone was very busy with the books. The bus moved into Harmilaap Nagar, where Gaurav Raheja lived. Vivek was waiting for him to come—for then they both again would discuss—"Have you studied something? Well! I have done nothing, and if you have done something, then please help me, too."

The bus stopped at the stop, the driver blew the horn, even after waiting for more than two minutes, Gaurav did not come. Vivek was feeling a bit worried for him, hence he requested the driver to wait more for a while. Nevertheless, he did not come and the driver after giving the last honk, started the bus, lest they could get late. They reached the school and while getting down from the bus, one junior student asked him— "It's also your examination today?"

He replied yes in a hurry and after best wishing him and everyone else in the bus, he moved towards the examination hall. There what he saw was one of the most shocking things he could ever see. There was no one present there from his class, but only juniors were sitting there. He re-checked the room number and got a bit more worried. He directly moved towards the teacher's room to ask about the sitting plan. He saw there his same chemistry exam teacher, who gave him admission to this school, and prompted to ask her about the same.

"What are you doing here, today?"

"Madam, it's your paper today—chemistry!"

She was in a funny mood for him for the first time; he could notice this on her.

"Oh sorry! Your chemistry paper is today! For rest of your classmates, it was yesterday only".

He was extremely shocked, so annoyed and ashamed of himself that he could not even notice the date-sheet of the examinations rightly. He was thinking why Gaurav did not call yesterday to ask about my non-appearance? Shocking! He was worried about telling his partents at home, or what if Gaurav would have called at home to ask about him in his absence, and his mother would tell him that he had gone to school to take chemistry exam? Whatever intuition Vivek was afraid of what had actually happened.

He had not visited Sonepat even once after getting admission to eleventh class, but once in his uncle's marriage for a night, when everyone got surprised at him there—now he was no more a child, but a boy with new soft whiskers. Even one of his grandmothers could not recognise him. It was surprising for him, too, as he was visiting the city after so many days, and that, too, during his semi-final examinations were going on. After that came the final examinations and his future was taking a quite strange turn again. He did not prepare for engineering entrance examination at all, which was necessary for getting admission in the Technical Institutes in India, but was a bit concerned about the IIT test, which was to be conducted by the IITs together, unknown to the fact that it was more difficult to clear and get admission to any of the IITs. Difficult because his mind did not work in the study fields though it was better in cricket or football.

Meanwhile, he indulged in these new fields; he was going far away from the thoughts of Laxmi, or forgetting her and according to his sister, "It was just attraction at its peak!"

He used to curse himself sometimes that; he went through such infatuation and was not destined for it finally, as everything God was giving him did not include her at all. So, he thought finally and asked the Almighty—

"Was it love?"

Moreover, he got the answer from his internal soul.

"If it was love, it was impossible for you to forget her like this. These experiences were just to make you clear about the meaning of the most thrilling feeling of living your whole life for someone who could be anyone. . . any. . . one!"

That time was the one when he was grooming up mentally, emotionally and physically. Most surprisingly, he now had headaches, he stressed his mind to bring out some meaningful thoughts and reasons for small things. The time of twelfth standard passed like anything and their farewell party was held, after a lot of requests and fake promises which the students made to the Principal, after their good results in the finals. The Farewell party stood though not such enjoyable, as some kind of disputes between students made it a regretting situation for all of them, who thought of enjoying the last moments together. Sometimes, a quarrel between two fools can bring a full stop to everyone's entertainment. How mean though! Well, they could only take some photographs with the cameras, they had brought for the occasion in that delicate situation. There were the board examinations, during which it was quite quiet as there were no more talks and fun with friends, but only serious studies for Vivek. As soon as the examinations were over, preparations for admission in a prestigious technical institute started. Then came the entrance examinations, out of which one test he took unprepared and the other one he appeared prepared to, went over-head, everything was unknown to him—his typical bad luck was prevailing. He gave his entrance examinations without the exact knowledge about the repercussions of failing in them, however, they were the examinations deciding future for every engineering aspirant.

Time between Twelfth and Engineering Admission

He got some important time, after giving the Board examinations and the entrance tests, and before the corresponding results declared. The Almighty was writing his further life in the best possible way for Him. Meanwhile, he decided to enjoy a bit and for the same he used to go to the play fields daily. As the result dates were approaching nearer, everyone except him was worried, as he could not win their trust in these two years, but he was sure that he will easily secure 60 per cent marks. When the twelfth class results were declared, unlike tenth class results, Vivek was with his whole family at home, as the date was confirmed. They were waiting for the results on computer. As soon as the result uploaded, the excitement was changing into fear. His family was afraid that he was going to fail or get very poor marks, which they will have to hide from family and friends, due to the competition with other children living even in the same apartments.

His father asked his roll number doubtfully as soon as the results were uploaded. As he rolled down the page whether the same roll number and name was there, he read something, which was more than a surprise for him. He rechecked the name and roll number, meanwhile his mother and sister were asking him to tell what happened! He said slowly— "English...80, Physical Science...80, Chemistry...65, Physics...62, and, and Mathematics...60! Daughter, isn't the sum around 70 per cent?"

In fact, he stood up in joy and hugged Vivek for the very first time since he was a baby, as per his memory. The feelings for him were inexpressible. He started telephoning every other friend of him asking their child's scores. However, this joy was short-lived, because the Entrance results were still to come. He could not qualify for the IIT entrance test and was able to score only 56 marks in the engineering entrance test. Moreover, for degree in Architecture, he got qualified for national counselling, which was good news for all of them. This news even shocked the school's principal, when he told her about it while taking his character certificate from there. She was very much surprised as Vivek was the second case, with such surprising news. One of their friends was selected in the IIT, who used to get marks like 'four out of 100' in mathematics and his attendance was the lowest.

However, his father did not want him to enter this field, as he had full faith on his son that he would never succeed in marketing. As Architect, mostly, one has to open his own office and work independently, and in that case, one has to be smart enough to attract the clients. Therefore, he had to enter the state counselling for admission in engineering institutes with a low score. He filled the choices of his own for the first counselling, which his father changed accordingly.

He wanted the mechanical programme, but his father wanted him to do computers, as everything is now done with the help of computers. However, the problem for Vivek was to find a way to convince that he was not ready for computers. Therefore, in the first counselling, he got admission in an institute which was under construction and he was not at all satisfied when his father sent him to see the working there. The day he went to see that institute, many things he learnt new— how the transport system of a state works and was lucky to see a very new place as well. That day, though his father directed him about the routes, he wanted to experience on his own, how to change the buses and auto-rickshaws to reach a particular destination himself. As if, he was on a mission to search his destination. He was amazed by everything there—the mountains, the clouds over them, the weather, the forests. Well, everything else a hardcore nature lover needs, to find in the nature. However, the main thing that day he was there for—the institute, was not in a satisfactory condition in any way. Neither the building was complete nor was the infrastructure. He was able to see so many things that day for the first time and realised that—'If you have the zeal to reach some destination and some properties are given by God to you, the people or again the Almighty's creations are so created, that they won't misguide you and help you reach your destination properly.'

Call it what you like, but that day also he reached the destination through the longest path he could follow. There were direct jeep or bus services to that place as told to him by his father, but he could get this, after travelling around that whole district. That whole day went in travelling and finding the institute, so he was a bit late in reaching back home. All the buses had left before he reached at the stop for Panchkula. At last, when he was feeling like crying at an unknown place, God knows, from where a jeep came and stopped nearby asking for the passengers for his home town.

He thanked God and was so happy that he got something to reach back home. It was around 8:45 in the night, when he reached home. There was another tour waiting for him. The tour, when his mother and father along with his sister, would shout at him for his hopeless mind, for not telling them about his proceedings. He was asking himself that time, that instead of asking about his whole day affair and the problems he had gone through in reaching back home, why they were shouting at him mere for not telling them about him during his outing? Now, he could understand that it was mistake not to inform them in time. The tension is really killing for the parents and it is our duty to tell them about our whereabouts. After sometime, they were cool enough to ask about the institute and he just opened the closed chapter of that institute in front of them—the poor condition of that institute in which he would never have gone. Therefore, now he had to fill his choices of institutes for the next counselling, hoping for the best. Through the next counselling, he got admission in the Technical Research Institute, again a new one, under construction, but with a much promising staff and the management. Therefore, they all decided to lend his future in the immature hands of this new institute. Vivek was a bit disappointed at first but soon realised that it had to set up itself and he would be one of the foundation students, so he had a lot of opportunity to help set up the institute in the line of famous engineering institutes. Their institute was so near to the Kurukshetra University, which affiliated it for a B.Tech degree in four branches, namely, Computers, Electronics, Information Technology and Mechanical. The initial days were a bit tough, but soon, he managed to live away from home, to fulfill his parents' wishes. In the first semester, as all the students were unknown to one another, so most of the time went in knowing each other, with light study. It was a great experience for him to recognise his friends and foes. He mostly used to stay alone in his own thoughts and always boosted himself to be stronger every day. He had to change his hostel many a time during the first semester because of the mismanagement of the people and the working staff. He learnt to eat the poor food. Soon the examinations came and as usual his Mathematics again played the lead role in his failure; his first engineering paper, Maths, performed very poor, and again he had a great start! Starting with a failure was becoming a crucial part of his life's curriculum.

3

THE CHANGE

TR Institute, Kurukshetra

Those were the early days of the second semester.They had got a new and worthy classroom, in front of the Director's office. All of the students knew each other. The institute was a newly established. They were a family, with petty disputes among them. Vivek was forgetting the loss of the Maths paper and was trying his best to concentrate on studies. He always tried to come back with a bang, in studies only. This was his habit that first he used to prepare a kind of time-table, in which he used to decide at least an hour for every subject. He could follow it only for one day strictly. He never knew who decided it for him, but he followed it whole-heartedly. It was the case with most of his friends. He sometimes asked himself—"I really don't know who has given us this right to decide time-table for us, when most of the things happening around are not in our hands? I have seen most of my teachers and famous people around the world, telling us regularly, to make a time-table. However, what is the output when you have to change it? I personally think that for us somebody else should prepare a time-table and keep a check on us for the same. Otherwise, if we prepare it ourselves, it is the tendency of human beings to become the greatest forgiver when it comes to their own mistakes."

For that amazing day in his life, the sun was shining brighter as if something good was going to happen. It was their physics lecture going on the early morning and he was sitting alone as usual in the class. Suddenly, he noticed that a guy, who didn't even talk to him in the whole first semester, was trying to approach him. Vivek knew him through Varun as the guy was Varun's roommate and Varun somehow did not like him as much. He did not know why, it was perhaps some ego problem about them. His name, Vivek did not ask, but he himself yelled in a different way. Started from— "Hello brother, can you answer my few queries?"

Vivek said—"Yes, why not?"

He looked excited and thrilled that day to sit with a poor guy, like Vivek, who was surprised to see such an excited personality that day. He asked some questions to which Vivek only answered— "Yes, of course!"

The questions were like—

"Could we get placed somewhere?", "Shall we be recognised by all?", "Would I be able to speak before a public?" and "Will somebody say—who did it" with a consequent answer—'of course, Siddhartha!' "Will I be a famous personality?"

Many more questions like that. He looked like a very hungry person, with every kind of dishes with him around—he possessed all of the qualities and still was searching for them outside. Vivek was also very happy to get someone who was so interesting and charming—the ever-green! However, he was a bit surprised that he sat with him asking such silly questions to him. As his first semester went in vain in search of a true friend, who could understand him, but soon he realised that "firstly, I have to become one like that."

Everyday seemed to be a new beginning for Vivek with Siddhartha, because of his so pomping behaviour. A fresh start everyday used to make him fresher because a person (Vivek), who was not so friendly according to others, had a friend now. Siddhartha used to behave like a child mostly. However, nobody would expect from a person with 6'2" height, to behave like that. However, a person who behaves childish is very grown up inside, that is, he had to hide his wisdom from the people, as they do not believe but argue. Siddhartha always used to discuss about the time spent in the college bus. All the other students in the bus used to curse Vivek for he was not a city guy as they were, to name him a '*desi kharaat*', though there were some who were his schoolmates also and supported him sometimes. The evil gets greater support nowadays. He agonised always and used to think about the ways how he could give them the lessons and thought that wearing the branded clothes could raise him to the same standard where the other students were. At that time, he was ignorant of the fact that neither it was required for a great person to be fashionable nor was compulsory for him to wear the branded clothes...and wearing branded clothes could not make him like them. It is a matter of adverse thinking only. At the first place, it was required to prove for them that he was also something. Some one really special in his own way. Siddhartha was not so mature to listen to Vivek that time. Therefore, Vivek used to support him for his branded stuff and used to show him that he was doing right in his place for he wanted support at that time. Being a friend if Vivek would have gone against his view, soon he would have become weaker. Vivek decided to make him stronger, but again needed time for that. Meanwhile, the studies were going smoothly and Vivek was gaining his confidence back, which was lost due to Mathematics paper in the first semester. Since he used to listen to him more, so now, Siddhartha was becoming friendlier with Vivek and used to share his tiffin with him instead with his other bus mates, who used to hurt them, as their victim was more independent of them now. They all showed it by commenting sometimes when they moved together. All were typical college people with a common thinking that they were superior to others as they were from a good city and a good family background. They all showed it. All nonsense! Vivek always tried to ask Siddhartha's views about these self- declared heroes and he always replied as if he was a slave to them, and was afraid of them in some way. Vivek was totally against this thing and used to boost him, that he was also something. He told him that they were proud of the things, they did not work hard to achieve, that is they were already rich as their parents were alive, and they were not equal to them in that sense at all. However, they will surely work hard and one day would get those things. Nevertheless, the main thing required for survival here on the mother earth was respect for all, love for all, and happiness in others' joy. They all lived in their own world of ego and hatred. Vivek was now getting positive signals from Siddhartha a guy, who would never give answers with mouth, but his deeds would thrill poor people, his busmates, even to think something negative about him. Moreover, they would have to stress their minds hard to get an idea Siddhartha was inferior to them.

In the second semester, nothing was going to be interesting anymore, as the examinations were coming near again. During the second sessional examinations, Siddhartha asked Vivek to have lunch with him onwards when he noticed that Vivek did not have lunch and he used to get away without it mostly. He was away from home. Vivek did not feel good but agreed to him thinking, he is asking with such a great heart, so who am I to denounce him from becoming great in my eyes?"

Vivek could feel his true feelings of giving his bit for him. Vivek did not agree for so many days because of his nature. He preferred giving more to taking. He soon realised that if everyone had such kind of nature, who would be left on the earth for whom we could do something? If all are going to be so independent, a time would come when no one would ask or expect anything from others, and there would be no respect for anyone in anybody else's heart. Therefore, an inter-dependency is must to let this world live in peace. As in India, earlier there used to be followed the barter system. If one has sugar, he would change it from the person having wheat grains and thus an exchange of goods and sharing of time together brought people more together. However, after the outsider's rule in India, these customs were forgotten and now we can see the fights between different people within the same country. Vivek had learnt from Vishakha that if you accepted gifts from the people who gave the gifts out of care, the acceptance helped in making them really satisfied at heart. The most expensive happiness we could give them with YES!

Therefore, he agreed to Siddhartha's request that he could now bring lunch for him as well. In this way, the bond of their friendship became stronger day by day. He got used to it in a few days though, thinking again and again that this was the Almighty who gives us every thing, and it can be bestowed through our parents or friends or relatives and even sometimes through the unknown people. This was the most surprising thing in this world, Vivek had noticed so far. You don't know someone and there is no connectivity, but still you can feel his/her pain, laugh on his stupid acts, weep watching his wounds and even start caring for him/her without his/her concern. The same was happening with Vivek and Siddhartha. Vivek used to be happy when Siddhartha did something good and Siddhartha was happy with his *stupid* talks. The most amazing thing in Siddhartha was his enthusiasm, which could even bind back a broken heart. Unknowingly, he was a pill for Vivek, too. He used to feel very alone earlier, but with him, he could at least share his knowledge and experiences. However, some experiences made him a bit more talkative, but Siddhartha enjoyed them until he had his own experiences, apace. Therefore, there was an inter-dependency between them, a mutual faderacy. A dependency, Vivek thought, was the only thing present in today's world, which could help in mutual bonding between all human beings and help increase the 'Peace Factor', one of the factors required for the improvement of the living atmosphere on mother earth. For Siddhartha an expression came in his mind and Vivek wrote it in his diary as:

> Met the unknown in the class,
> A person transparent like a glass,
> Excited much more about his life,
> About work, job, his wife,
> Immature he wanted prominent his part,
> Everywhere scripted his name—SIDDHART!
> Known are a per cent out of hundred,
> He wanted but to be a head,
> Determination was high and with him a God,
> In fight of life, he bade a nod.

One thing Vivek could notice in Siddhartha was his greatest zeal to become a person highly qualified, with higher degrees like Ph.D. He wished to be a businessman, or a teacher, who could bring about some positive changes in the world. A teacher always participates in the future of a nation through his/her students. He was a good orator as known to Vivek; from the day he met him. But Siddhartha was unknown of his qualities. He could handle any stage of this world of any size earlier, due to his acute eagerness and talent. As the time passed, Vivek observed that this eagerness of becoming well-known was the most important quality in Siddhartha, which he could use in a very positive manner. Vivek was a very poor student since childhood. Getting 80 per cent of marks in tenth standard was the only good score through his certificates. His feelings used to well up sometimes, as he always said:

"Being in love, I was perfect. Now see, how poor my situation is in every field. Neither I study nor do I feel love in the surroundings. So boring is life without love. Why am I here, man? There is nothing here that ignites me to do something for a change."

On the other hand, Siddhartha was one of the toppers of the institute, and he used to help Vivek in his studies. This way, he stole his heart and after making a place for himself, turned it back to him. One of the instances, Vivek always remembered about the hidden greatness in Siddhartha. There was their Electronics paper the next day and he called Vivek up on the phone asking him about his preparations. Vivek had replied—

"Nothing so far, just nothing".

Vivek was not much tensed but Siddhartha was. He asked him about the notes of some important topics, which he did not have. He now was more concerned and asked him— "OKAY! Just tell me what do you have?"

After knowing about the stuff Vivek had, on the very phone for more than one and a half hour, Siddhartha taught him and helped him prepare for at least 60 marks. He made the call only for his benefit, wasted such a precious time and hooked his eyes in the candle light on the occasion in absence of electricity. Vivek cleared that paper easily. Selflessness, though a mystery, is a great thing given to human beings by the Almighty. The only thing, which used to confuse Vivek, was— "What is there in me that made him talk to me and befriend me? I am actually of no use to anyone; however, I have a heart to fill with love for people I meet and know. So, I should try my best to help him in my best way possible."

Vivek never thought, there was any compatible quality in him that could match with so many qualities Siddhartha had. He was a person with a zeal to love while Siddhartha was a person with zeal to work. This was the reason he realised later, which was responsible for their meeting. Distribution of both these properties was required for the survival of both of them and Vivek believed that it was also required for the survival of this world and the different people living in it. One could never have all the properties in oneself, otherwise one will not ask someone else for other things and will start living for oneself only. However, if we were to live much independently, a different earth was required for everyone. Dependency is the thing, which inspires us to have a healthy relationship with each other. Vivek used to hear in his childhood from his grandparents and his mother about the life earlier in their country. How forefathers were so peaceful and loving in the folds of nature.

"They used to share their individual assets. A peasant used to give grains to a doctor to get himself cured. Two real brothers used to have a mutual understanding about their common land and used to do divided hard work and then share the output and lived happily in unity. In addition, our society was divided into different castes and religions according to their individual works. Like, a person cutting hairs was named 'barber' and a person using hacksaw to cut wood into furnitures was named 'carpenter', but nowadays, our society believes that these things define the standard of a person and look down upon them as poor people and hence the feelings for each other are no more. There is no respect in our eyes for the person, who produces our food grains, builds our houses, designs our furniture, makes the shoes for us to wear. The person who weaves our clothes or the person who drives trains, drives it with full responsibility even at late night, so that we reach home in time. Do we think about his/ her well being? No! Because we are so contained in ourselves and our problems that we don't find time for somebody else's problems."

Thinking these things in mind, Vivek used to be so

angry on himself that he cursed his luck for the times he lost, but now realised that he got the choice to concentrate his mind on different things also, about which most of us were unknown. That is why he took the problems of his friend Siddhartha as his own and in this way; he could forget his own problems. This way we can even minimise most of our problems by sharing.

One day Siddhartha came to his hostel room, and saw him doing some push-ups.

"How to do these? I want to do them, too!"

"You need strong feelings and zeal to do that, dear."

"What kind of feelings?"

"Oh! dear, you will not understand at present. You need to love in order to grow."

"Then how can you do that? If you can do so, I can try as well. What sort of feelings?"

Vivek smiled at him and said bringing his romantic feelings out again— "Well dear, I started it because I felt the importance of strength in a relationship, though for me it go one sided. It was a strong feeling and used to increase daily, which inspired me to start that exercise every day in my tenth standard. Well, leave it. You will not understand this. I will tell you about it after sometime, when you would feel the same about a girl. But, don't worry, I will let you wait till then. I know how important it is for you at present."

Vivek told him to try out one himself, but he could not do even once and his whole body was trembling, as he had never tried it earlier. It was a sort of '*desi*' exercise, which one could perform only with practice. Then he again did some and this was enough to ignite Siddhartha. Now he decided that he, too, would do this exercise and become stronger in any case. Vivek told him to start with five push-ups a day and then gradually if he moves up to 50 per day, it would surely make him stronger. That was the day, which changed Siddhartha's views of himself, of being a weak person. He was sure now that if he would practise, he would surely succeed in gaining good strength and be powerful physically to counteract his bus mates also. However, he was required to show his strength at a handshake only. Siddhartha was becoming stronger and stronger day by day and used to have lots of *soyabean* for high protein input and for quicker growth, which was required after heavy exercise. His physic improved drastically within a few weeks and he was then, called 'body-builder'– in the college. This was one of the experiences with Vivek which he could share with him. A few things Siddhartha used to ask from Vivek. As one day, he saw him hitting the wall of his hostel room with his punch and asked— "What will happen if I try this out, too?"

Vivek told him that this was just to make your grip better. Moreover, after that, he used to try it as Vivek did.

Vivek found that to attaining fame was not a problem but a need for a person who has some gift or talent bestoward by God, which could bring people together for a cause. Siddhartha also had a passion of doing something great for the people around him. He could teach the poor students with quality, who cannot afford to pay high standard institutes. In addition, he wanted to provide employment to as many people as he could. Therefore, Vivek thought this was the internal power, which sometimes made him so active and seemed to other an over-reaction. However, Vivek could now understand this was not his problem but a duty he had to perform as directed by the Almighty. In this way, Vivek could meet another person in his life who was going to become a well-known personality, after his schoolmate Gaurav Raheja, whom many people knew during the school time. The reason was his friendly nature and when the system of micro blogging websites came into existence, it was clear from his long list of friends not only from *Bharat* but from outside as well. Well, he was a storehouse for all friends, as all the friends could trust him for keeping their individual secrets. Vivek learnt a lot from him. He also taught Vivek, how to remain cool and relaxed, even when there was tension around. Another thing he learnt from Gaurav was to involve oneself in the happiness of others. Another friend of Vivek, Sahil Bansal, used to spend most of the money on their 'get togethers', just for the sake of his friends' happiness. His two best friends from the early school days—Manjeet and Nitish taught him to help others with all one had and not to cheat anyone in life. They both taught him and never gave their notebooks to him, to copy the homeworks. However, due to this reason, he got punishment many times. However, when he used to ask them the reason for not helping him, they replied *in lemine*— "If we give you the notebooks and you complete the homework so easily, you'll never learn to do it yourself. If you ask, we could explain all the topics. But, you will have to do the exercises yourself!"

These teachings by them were still in his mind so fresh and he kept on telling others about it, so that they could change their nature of selfishness and be a bit more humane.

He now wanted to share all these experiences with his friend Siddhartha, unknown of the fact that he might have known all this, but just to do his little bit for him. By this, one most important thing he wanted to share was—his Romantic views. The most common question Vivek used to ask everyone was "Have you ever loved a girl? You know how does it feel like?"

As if he wanted to indulge himself in their love stories and wanted to be a part of it. However, most of the times he used to control his feelings thinking people would make fun of them.

Meanwhile, Siddhartha kept bringing lunch for Vivek as usual while Vivek kept on returning the favour by telling him the ways to fight the cursing people in his life or the proud people with him. Vivek had learnt from his grandfather and parents not to forget the deeds of someone done for us, in any case. Especially the food you have with the blessings of someone must be in our thoughts always, even if that person is against us now. He did his bit for us and for the whole life; we should remain obliged to him for that. For this reason Siddhartha became a part of Vivek's daily life in the college and slowly their friendship grew robust. This is how a person completely unknown to him earlier was someone closer to his heart now. There is greed of some kind behind the first conversation between two strangers. However, if we keep the greed aside, it is a new relationship in making a friendship. This is the journey of life, where you do not know where to go, whom to meet, whom to befriend and whom to trust. Still new people come in our lives, make a space for themselves and remain there always then after. So, how could we hate someone when we do not know him/her exactly? This could never be in our hands, he thought. For example, one day he saw two of his college friends fighting beastly for a very poor reason of 'self respect' and for this reason, they were ready even to kill each other. However, see what was in the Almighty's store for them. One of them was injured badly in an accident and the other one was coming from behind and after seeing that somebody has been hurt in an accident, he was ready to help him (without knowing who he was). Wow...! They were fighting two days back and now, one was taking the other to the hospital. Both live happily now and together, as if they were never indulged in any fight. If this little thing we all understand, how wonderful and amazing this world would look! We mostly live selflessly, for others. For example, a father works so hard for his children to brave them food. A mother wakes up for whole night when her children are ill, a friend is ready to give whole of his money to save his mate in case of an accident. A night watchman wakes up for the whole night and keeps on roaming around the society, keeping his life at stake for all of us. However, this is the mistake we do, start giving reasons behind the things. Why could not we be natural enough to live for others and not being that much selfish? Why do we have reasons for everything we do not want to do? If somebody wakes us up at two at night, we start hating him/her, without knowing the reason behind this. Well, in today's world the main problem is, we know everything and the ways to implement the things but do not do so, just to satisfy ourselves. Vivek's grandfather used to ask sometimes in anger— "What is this self-respect actually? How can a person respect himself? What will be the outcome of respecting oneself?"

He once taught Vivek— "A person could only be respected for his good deeds and that too by others. Nobody in this world, whom you hurt anyhow is going to respect you. It is a thing that is earned for the whole life slowly and slowly, and lost with a blink of eye. So, son, give it all you have to help someone and earn respect from his heart in return, not the flattering or buttering words from his mouth".

4

THE KNIVES AND SWORDS

Their life was going very interesting in the college and in the hostel also. They used to enjoy all the moments to the fullest as if this was the only period, they could enjoy for the rest of their lives. The semesters were passing very swiftly and a very little time was left for them, in the institute. However, in between there were some unforgettable experiences. One of them was becoming a part of the amazingly innovative team— "The Re-Invigorators...are bringing new energy !" An industrial trip was organised for their institute to Vivek's birthplace—Sonipat and this innovative team was given the charge of discipline there, with Vivek and Siddhartha as the co-ordinators of the team, and other eleven friends as the mentors over the junior students. In addition, this was an innovative team, there were so many ideas with them and they implemented most of them to make the trip worth remembring. They decided to be in time everywhere and though this was odd for most of the people in Hindustan, who were used to getting late, including Vivek's father that day. They had decided to wear the dress code of white shirt with black pant and shoes with their institute coat. In addition, they distributed batches amongst every junior which they had donned for easy recognition. Vivek shared this experience as that day was special for them. Though they were official co-ordinators, they also had the authority to take any step against the culprit students, who were notorious in nature. According to the disciplinary norms decided by all of the Re-innovators if a student was found below the norm in one industry, he/she would not be allowed to enter the next one and had to sit in but the bus. One case Vivek remembered was of two brothers, who were creating disturbance in the bus, though allowed but not in the industrial area, the report came to them as they were standing before the industry with their respected HOD. The mentor told the co-ordinators about the problem and the students thought to seek some help from their HOD. The HOD directly said that the control that day was not in his hands and asked Vivek and Siddhartha to taking a decision. That moment Vivek could see for the first time, the great leadership quality in Siddhartha, the way he handled the situation and taking them strictly as was decided. This made him and all the mentors feel proud as well. At last, there was a seminar and again all were spell bound by the discipline and the answers from them all.

After that day, Vivek was sure now Siddhartha was a stronger person from inside as well. A man with a height above 6'2" was now ready to handle any position anywhere in this world. He was now physically as well as mentally a stronger person Vivek could see easily. That day was the building stone in the future of at least all those thirteen of the Re-innovators, because they were now experienced of organising an event and maintaining discipline for its success as well. After that, they got appraisal from the management of the institute well. The list of all those thirteen students was kept for future assistance by the administration of the institute. They celebrated that trip silently for a reason that this was just a start and miles were to go still, no matter a milestone was achieved or not.

Celebrations on Siddhartha's Birthday, Kurukshetra

As Siddhartha was a known personality now in the whole institute, so all decided to celebrate his birthday with all the persons known to them invited in the party. They decided to collect some money altogether to make it a big day worth remembering. A Disk Jockey was arranged for the event and a permission was taken from all the neighbours out there. Again, this was an event, which inspired everyone to say that "Siddhartha! You are different from others, as no other student could think of arranging such a grand party except you and inviting everyone like that!"

That day Vivek danced from heart and just got mad like anything and kept saying— "Dancing is not an act, which you can do on somebody's request. If you are happy in somebody else's happiness you will dance without any DJ and if not, you will keep on giving silly reasons only like 'I am sorry, I don't know how to dance!'

It made him feel laugh at heart to see people pretending to be happy for others, when their hearts were burning actually to see the happiness of others. He kept dancing that night in a very different way, just in his own way till the DJ stopped playing music and it was a mystery that why he was telling Siddartha to make a video of him about the same, saying that—"Make a video of mine like that. You never know, in future you will be able to see me like that or not! I feel like dancing to the limit today. Might be this video helping in your marriage. For reasons, if I would not be able to attend it, you could play this video and feel my presence. You can show your wife that there used to be a silly friend of yours like me."

A few days later, as they all were in the second last semester of their Engineering course, everybody was busy with their interviews and so were Vivek and Siddhartha.

Knife of the Lord for Him

One day, Siddhartha phoned Vivek and told him that he had a surprise for him, which he will tell him, only if he will visit him personally. Vivek got the idea somehow about the surprise that he would have got a job and in that joy and excitement, he just started as quickly as he could on a motor bike to meet him. In the way, as he was thinking about how they would celebrate the moment and whom to include in the party and whom not, something serious happened. Moreover, as if the destiny was taking him towards itself and out of excitement he was driving at a bit higher speed than normal, however, carefully. Suddenly, he did not remember what happened and he lost his balance in that excitement.

He met with a big accident. His eyes opened in the hospital only and that too after five days as told to him by the nurse there. He saw around and could see an oxygen cylinder installed on him, the nurse and the doctors. All were looking at him, as if he was to tell them about the secret locker with the highest amount in the world. He asked them if he could meet anyone from his family or friends. They called in Siddhartha, who was waiting outside for his consciousness. Vivek asked him about his parents and he told him that his father had gone to take medicines and mother had gone to take their dinner from home.

"Okay!"

He then tried to get up, as he was feeling very uneasy lying constantly there, but was unable to use his hands and legs as they were not moving. He got perturbed and asked Siddhartha— "What is happening? Why am I unable to move my legs and the hands? Are they tied up? I am feeling as if a lot of weight has been put on my legs."

As soon as he asked him, Siddhartha broke down. He started weeping with his heavy head heaving on Vivek's chest. He could not get anything from it but was in a state of some tension after seeing him burst like that for the first time. He asked in anger now—

"For God sake tell me! What happened?"

The reply from Siddhartha took everything from Vivek and left him blank from any kind of thoughts for a while. He had lost all his legs and hands in the accident. However, he had his brain and mouth working, he could tell his problem and someone had to help him in getting his work done. That moment the Lord answered to the query he had in his mind about why he was telling Siddhartha to make a video of him dancing that day, as he would never dance like that in future any more. That video was to remind him, about his great past, about his casual behaviour and the way he danced out of joy. He now understood that we get the signals before the incident happens, the only mistake we do is we ignore them. This was the knife; he got out of shock from the Almighty.

Sword of the Lord for Him

He used to say a set of lines to himself, whenever he used to fail in his examinations or something bad happened with him—

> Today I have fallen, tomorrow I will rise,
> Think, this failure will surprise,
> This world is full of problem and test,
> But I'll emerge the best!

This was a bit more bitter situation for him to adjust in. However, what else he could do. Soon his—'Never give up, there is a light somewhere!'—nature brought him back and he said— "I have lost only, not died yet! What happened if I have a set of paralysed hands and legs? I will live to the fullest still with your help if you give me."

He asked Siddhartha— "At least now tell me what the

surprise was! See! I have given such a tough test to know about it!"

What he told was the same Vivek thought it to be. He had got a job in a well renowned multi-national company with a very high salary, which was enough for him to fulfill all his dreams. Siddhartha got answers to all his queries he asked Vivek when they met for the very first time in the Physics lecture, in second semester of their Engineering. Vivek could remember that they both used to think about owning one big car and a bike with great thump someday. Now, all those dreams would accomplish soon. Vivek thanked God that at least his memory was safe though he took everything else from him. He could remember the joyous moments of his life, though he could not live them again. To feel what went with him, a mind was must and to come up from that situation a positive thinking was required. Vivek was thankful to God that day, that Siddhartha got a job. However, Siddhartha was more concerned about Vivek's situation at that time. Vivek just piled up all his feelings into a small poem—

> Shocked was I, thinking why I got this life?
> I asked God why for me he decided this knife.
> All my dreams were shattered into pieces!
> My love, my power fails, displeases!
> But stressing on my mind I got the reason,
> A life whole left to live for someone,
> I only had thoughts to help the other,
> As farmer, as brother, as mother!
> This is life—full of ups and downs!
> It happens to the brighter crowns!
> One is to be determined and keep his faith burn,
> This is the way, great people are born!

He was hospitalised in a very good hospital at his birthplace, and was to live there for the rest of his life. Moreover, the staff there was very nice and the nurse was really very helpful in nature as he could now write his story with her help. She used to keep sitting there in the absence of Siddhartha and his parents. She used to hear his story and write it for him. He now decided to be a writer with the nurse as his hand and adjusted himself in that kind of atmosphere. After a few days, Siddhartha joined the company and Vivek told him to be regular there and come to him only if he got lessuire. However, Siddhartha used to come to him every day. He used to tell him about his whole day, as if Vivek, too, was a part of his office, and on a leave for few days. He used to go back only after one of the persons from Vivek's family came there. Vivek had a fixed daily routine, as he had to lie permanently on that bed only. However, most of the time there used to be people around him. He used to feel guilty of himself sometimes, that because of him, those people were bound, but the concept of dependency used to come to his mind and get him out of those weird kinds of thoughts. His friends and relatives never allowed him to feel lonely or let him think about his illness at all. Those kind people and his positive approach were the swords of the Lord given to him to fight his helplessness.

5

THE EXCITEMENT

After Siddhartha joined his office and Vivek got admission in the hospital, the life became a bit busy for Siddhartha. However, Vivek was totally free to think, listen, read and see the things, which other people do not have time for. He had the most precious thing with him for these things, which others normally do not have—Time! His daily life was congested and everything was mostly for sure to happen for him. His parents along with his sister used to arrange shift for his friends, to stay in the Hospital for taking care of him. He was now thinking of getting rid of this kind of weird situation anyhow. He was perturbed to see everyone related to him like that and could realise that a life without any organ is so difficult to live and how hard it was to sustain in this world for a handicapped. However, determination helps them to do most of the things like others, but 'a heart only can understand the feelings of another heart, a mind cannot.'

He could now feel about being so dependent on others for his whole life and felt very bad to see the people coming to ask about his health. Most of his friends came there to ask the same question repeatedly and he had no replies other than— "I am fine! Trying my best to indulge myself in a life, dependent on others."

This indirectly also helped him take his mind off his health and think about others' issues.

He usually used to ask Siddhartha about the conveyance, by which he used to come to see him, as he was against the use of own car when the public transport system was so active. Siddhartha earlier used to oppose him, as they both had some dreams of owning big cars and bikes, but now after getting the resources actually and understanding that it was more important to save the mother earth from pollution and stuff like that, they both were not so interested in either of the things, *though they owned them.* As Vivek used to be free for whole of the day when all others used to go to work, he had time to think about their individual problems and sometimes about some social issues like, how to change the poor things happening around by doing our bit? The main problem which was there as he could hear from the nurse, was the increasing temperature outside due to pollution and the waste material or garbage lying here and there, implicting so many diseases and also the foul smell coming out of it. This always perturbed him and compelled him to think over so such self-centred and selfish nature of Human Beings. Sometimes, he felt so depressed and angry that he tried to push his nerves, to move his body but all in vain. How easy is this, to think that we throw the waste material or garbage outside, only satisfying our mind that at least our own house is clean and disease-free, but why do we forget that the world outside is also ours. It's we all, who have also to use those resources—the streets, the roads, the pipelines, the fresh air *that comes travelling through different places whether clean or not.* How easily we curse others about the same when they do it. Vivek always stressed use of buses and used to get annoyed when Siddhartha used to come by his car.

He used to think about what are the things, which are in our hands and which are not. Where he was to take birth in India or somewhere else in this big world? When he was to take birth? When he was to learn the way to talk or walk? When he was able to think for the very first time or when he was able to judge something, as good or bad! Why he was not able to grow up immediately? Why we are born and why we die? Why today his situation was like this? All these and many other questions, for which he could never get satisfactory answers. It was also a kind of mystery for him to know why someone feels to be good and someone to be bad! However, after so much thinking and stressing on his mind to extract the answers, he was able to know—"a *big zero*—which is also the point from where we came into existence! Everything else was just an assumption as a whole. Dimensions are actually assumptions only, *where some starting point and then an end point is taken.* But, how we can assume something, if the universe is unlimited? Where is this earth located? Is it at the centre of the universe? But how there could be any centre, when this universe is unlimited? Vivek used to smile asking these questions to himself and sometimes the Nurse. One day he asked the Nurse— "Sometimes I feel pity on these *limiters*, who try to put restriction to imagination and give dimensions to different things. This is a country named India, then there is a border and after it is Pakistan or Nepal. I mean, is there any border physically present between these different countries, dear sister?"

"No dear, borders were made after the separation. Otherwise, it was just like you move freely in states in your own country", nurse replied.

"Okay! So, these borders are also a result of some thinkers, who thought that dividing the land would bring happiness around and all the people believed the thoughts of those thinkers and started living accordingly. I think, this is some supernatural power giving these instructions to those people, who think so much about peace and humanity. Otherwise, there was only one result—people would have fought and ultimately died. Though, the same *death* is the ultimate thing. However, our ancestors gave it up to a negative thinking, that if different people stay together, they would fight among. Well, I still salute the negative thinkers, as their thoughts were believed. Perhaps be there was no positive thought of Love or peace, which could make people surrender to itself that time."

He continued—"Man was born naked; he made clothes to cover and to save himself from effects like wind, sun etc. Everything evolved out of some kind of need. Need to share the thoughts, need of people to complete a family, need of customers for a businessman, need of a female to give birth to the next generation, need of health to live more, need of money to own a big house, car, etc. When these needs are accomplished, we feel satisfied and this gives us happiness. We even need 'a need', to be happy! We need to give something to get something back. There is a bond between everyone here on this earth, somehow. Then, why our ancestors could not understand the same? Religion is what a group of people follow, as in earlier times, God had to visit in different forms to preach-peace and love. But today, I think technology has made everything as one. Still some hopeless minds believe that any particular Religion is the greatest. All religions, however, teach to reach a single point, only the ways to reach can be many different. You can not announce a particular religion as greater than any other. I mean at least think before you believe people!"

"Oh Son! Calm down. Nobody else than me is listening!", said the sister.

"No. This is what you don't understand. I am expressing feelings out in my own way and the same will be acknowledged somewhere ...someday. I am sure about it.", he was as confident as ever.

Vivek continued— “Still, Isn’t it amazing, sister? If I have done something great, I have to share it with everyone, to feel the greatness. Similarly, I need more customers to increase my business. Our science also needs people to see, cherish, use or experience its great inventions and discoveries”, You know sister, this thinking gave me the answer about one thing for sure—why do we love?”

“And may I know, what the answer is Mr. Thinker?” sister asked Vivek, while taking out his medicines from the box, kept on the table at the corner of his bed.

“We love each other to care, to learn something new, to teach, to feel, to be happy, to be known, to be felt by someone and finally to exist. To hate someone even, we need to love someone else, whether it is oneself. Even the most dangerous animal loves itself and hence attacks its predators. People say, The fittest or the strongest survive’ However, why we need to survive? To hate someone? Or to kill someone and ultimately die? Why don’t we think before hating someone that he might be in love too, like us, or somebody else might be loving him/her?”, Vivek still was trying to explain his sentence while the sister interrupted, “And why do we care?”

“We care for our existence. We exist because somebody cared, now we will care and somebody else will exist. If I understand the fact that I exist, not because of myself but because of somebody else and not for myself but for somebody else, it clears all my doubts. So, when we understand this truth about relativity—we care”, answered Vivek with closed eyes.

There was complete silence when he finished, which compelled him to open his eyes. Sister was looking at him smiling.

“One thing is for sure, you lying in the bed just think and think. Am I right? You have got this good job of thinking for everyone”

"No... It is not so, I just wanted to...!" Vivek had tried to hide his shyness, and they laughed.

"This means that I even cannot share my feelings now, because everyone would say, 'these are the thoughts of an empty mind, which has nothing to do with realities', said Vivek teasing the sister.

The sister requested him, "Don't stress your mind that hard, or it will burst out in vain!"

However, Vivek used to think, even if, he doesn't do anything, he has to die in vain and tried to give his heart some condolence— "At least I can try my level best to think something positive and extract something effective from my idle mind, which I would share with my sister or tell my parents or Siddhartha's to feel relaxed, so that they would tell others about it and I am sure the generated feelings will not go waste. It is about the strong determination behind any thought. If a negative thought could change that much of the society, just think, how much the positive thought would do. I know it is a boring topic for you to discuss. However, I firmly believe that you yourself will discuss this topic (*Love*) someday, with yourself or with someone else."

He thought to write a poem at that point of time.

I have a problem, I cannot tell others about,

Neither I can scream nor can I shout,

Why it is happening all around?

Hatred among people—in water, sky, on ground!

I am unlucky that I can only think and keep quiet!

As I know, there is no difference between black and white!

But, how should I make others understand?

As I have neither proofs nor some glands (body parts)!

He had no work to do in the hospital, or rather one could say that even if he had work, he couldn't do it with his hands and legs paralysed. What else was left for him then? Either think, or sleep! Vivek wanted some work, to keep him busy and resist the thinking, which used to make him frustrated. Why there was so hatred even after so much dependencies? Sometimes, it feels like he rightly said, "*Meditation* is the work of an empty mind, *free of tensions and negative thinking* and we should try that once at least, as it helps us getting hidden answers of the common questions we have."

Vivek being a romantic fellow used to feel love for others most of the times and used to smile on what he used to do when he was fine. In the next room, there was a girl admitted, who had lost her right arm in an accident and her husband used to stay there most of the times. Vivek used to watch them silently caring for each other. One day, the sister asked him, "Why do you keep looking at them like that?"

Vivek taking a deep breath said,

"I feel what they feel. They both care for each other like anything. Look at her husband. He keeps serving his wife with care, medicines, food, water and everything. He shares everything with her and she listens to whatever he says patiently. She sometimes feels that he is doing a lot for her and tries to stop him doing something rigorous. I have never seen them fighting. They are in love with each other, as they are with least number of complaints. Sometimes I think, what shall Laxmi think about me if she sees me like that?"

"Who is Laxmi? Your girlfriend?"

"No sister. She is the one to teach me how to give all unknowingly. She never did anything for me directly, but indirectly, as an unknown, she has assigned me a great task of understanding love to the depth. I was thrilled even to think, that I saw her with my own eyes, in this life. I wanted to tell her everything but could never tell her about it. I used to play with my feelings. I always tried to generate feelings as if they were directly moving into her heart and thought that she would come to me one day, hug me and say—'Oh! Why you did that? Why do you love me so much? You know how difficult it is, to resist the true feelings', but nothing has happened so far. Still, I believe in my heart that the story you are writing for me will reach her and she would someday come to see me, although I shall die and feel proud that I loved her. I think that feelings of any kind do not go waste. God takes care about it."

"Oh! Deep Thinker is a deep lover as well. Interesting", Sister looked at him with her eyebrows raised.

"Well, you know it happens. There is nothing to hide. I never did it from my end. I never started it actually. That was just an accident and I am still thankful to my dear friend Sumer. If he had not complained to me, I would have never seen such a beauty. God plays a lot with his little bodies and souls." There was a smile on his face, as he said so.

He believed firmly that there was some supreme power, still unknown to most of us, doing all the things. Nevertheless, the selfishness of humans perturbed him the most as he used to say,

"We know that trees give us oxygen, but still we are cutting them. Why? Either to earn more or for our livelihood! Nevertheless, why we don't let them grow at individual level and stop waiting for something miraculous to happen! We know that diseases spread because of dirt and garbage still we throw the wastes in the streets, inside the trains and in others' houses. What do we want actually? love or hatred for all? peace or disturbance for all? construction or destruction for all? We demand more and pay less. Why?"

Siddhartha used to calm him down sometimes by nodding yes to his frustration because he knew that it was not good for his weak nervous system.

"Yeah, I know that you are right. But please, try to understand, that nobody is here to listen to your deep thoughts. Don't worry. Everything would be fine, if you improve yourself. First of all, fight against your illness and then fight for others' illness or *recoupment*."

"Yes, but see. Everybody wants to be healthy without any physical exercise and eating unhealthy stuff. Everyone wants care and love without loving others, instead they seek love and care at the cost of hating others. The new generation wants time for themselves and even think of their parents as disturbing elements. What will they do in that emptiness—think, smoke, drink, talk to walls and whatever they think of doing alone, there is an indulgence of something else. Then, why, why we try mostly to live for ourselves? This dependency, I can only feel, when the sister writes my poems. What I am giving to her? I am just a duty for her but out of Human she writes what I dictate.

"Okay! Calm down. Let's discuss something else", Siddhartha again tried to change his mind.

"It's Okay! One thing I wish, if somebody could help me with it".

"What?"

"Nothing man, you do not understand these feelings. I just wanted that if someone could inform Laxmi about the immense love buried deep in my heart for her, after I die."

"Not again, please dear lover"

Siddhartha was not that romantic, however, he had some beliefs in his those kinds of non-stop talks and he used to listen to Vivek for late nights, sometimes. Vivek knew that *mostly they were out of care, otherwise who has time for these kinds of talks today*; as everybody is so busy with his/her life. Perhaps they were a part of their true friendship. Vivek had a lot of respect and satisfaction for Siddhartha for this reason specially. Siddhartha was also selfless in taking care about Vivek and lending his ears to him for his 'stupid' and most of the times boring talks.

The days went by like this and one day the doctor told Vivek about another problem, which had occurred inside his body, as a part of that accident. His bone marrow was shrinking due to his non-moving body and it was incurable, if he himself didn't become active.

"Listen carefully Vivek. I find only you as the 'brave-hearted' person in your family. Your mother starts crying, even when I approach her to tell that you are fine. Your father already is a heart patient and your sister is another emotional person, I find. You were brave, even when you heard that your body is paralysed.

It was a normal thing for Vivek, though he wanted to live for a while to see his friends settling down and marrying happily. As he always had a dream to dance in their marriages before the '*Ghori*', typical Indian style of marriages, when the *dulha* or the bridegroom, sits on the back on a female horse and moves toward, the bride's place. However, as he could not even stand, what to think of dancing? It was so harsh but he accepted it happily, as he would not be a priority for anyone anymore and they would be free from taking care of a living 'dead' body. He wanted to tell this to Siddhartha first, as he had full faith in him, that he would take care of his parents after his death. He wanted to consolidate them in better bonds slowly, before his death, so that they would feel the loss less. He also had decided to tell him some points in the context.

Sister saw him thinking about the same and interrupted, "So, you think it's over?"

"What?" Vivek said bringing his concentration to what was asked by Sister.

"The so-called love?" asked the nurse sister again.

"Oh dear Sister, it is forever. It will never end and increase more with time. Yes, I know life has an end attached to it. But, why to worry? Life should be the motto, rather than complaining about its end. See, I loved a girl, I did not tell her about it and she will never feel it. However, this will never change the truth that she gave me those feelings, whether unknowingly. I am satisfied that I could feel that feeling once and forever, due to her. She gave me the experience and knowledge, which is absent in most of the people".

"Why don't you try to find her and do the last good thing by expressing your views to her?"

Vivek smiled and said, "Let destiny decide, what it has in store for me now! But one thing, I would like to share with you".

"Sure dear. Go ahead". said the sister.

"These feelings are really very heavy to carry. Your surroundings make it difficult to stand with your beliefs intact. Situations try to compel and change the way you think about loving each other. But that is where comes your 'UGO.'"

"What is UGO?", interrupted the sister.

"UGO is the positive of EGO. Your UGO will increase the love in you and help you increase it further. It will also help you become loyal to your feelings and ultimately to the person you love. Being loyal to the thought even that 'I am Loyal' is your UGO."

"How do you elaborate this?" asked sister again.

"Let me share an example with you here. You love your husband and simply love him. Ok! I wish it never happen though, but assume that he does not love you much and this hurts you. Your expectations and ego will hurt you for this. However, your UGO will help heal all the pain. You have to believe it firmly that you love him and stick to it no matter what happens. It was you to believe it earlier as well, that you are in love with him. You gradually decrease your personal desires and learn that your body will not last forever. You will also make yourself capable of bearing huge amounts of pain like this. Now, you will say-'What is God doing then?' He remembers that you said to yourself that you love him and is now checking your patience. 'Why he needs to check?' The answer again is very simple—'Everything is moving towards its end but it is your duty to take care of the things generated inside you and the same follows for your love'. So, your UGO tells you to continue even in the most weird situations."

"But, why we have to compromise in love always?" asked sister.

"Who says that? It is mere a thought. See it positively. When in love, you even love to give whatever you have to your beloved. Do you call it a compromise, when you intentionally give your things to someone? The sacrifice that gives you happiness is not at all a compromise. You compromise in the things, you do not own. If you do not love someone and have to do something for him is a compromise. When you love someone, you are dependent on him/her for love. If he or she loves less than you do, it means he/she is compromising", elaborated Vivek.

"But are not you compromising keeping all the love for Laxmi inside?"

"I know, I am. Nevertheless, this book will help me overcome this compromise, too. I believe she will enjoy this hidden romance, I had with her."

Vivek's sister Drishti heard him talking to sister about Laxmi, when she was entering his room. She thought for a while with an 'An... ha...', and continued standing outside to hear their complete conversation.

"Whose talks are going on? And, who is this Laxmi, I must know?" she thought standing outside.

Meanwhile, the nurse sister started interrogating Vivek about his love.

"Tell me please. What kind of a girl was she and how you fell in love with her?"

"But why do you want to know this sister?" asked Vivek.

After a while, he started telling her his love story, bringing out his burried feelings-

"Okay...Her name is Laxmi and she was my junior in Goddess Saraswati School. She was in Ana's class. She took the most precious thing, my soul. I used to enjoy my madness at that time as I still do. She took my mind and soul and never returned it back '*They are, her properties actually*'. I saw her because of my friend Sumer, when we were sitting in the activity hall where he asked me to ask her to remove her knee brush from his knee.

However, I have nothing much to boast about as I have not seen her for last seven years now. Still, if I close my eyes and think, I can easily recall her beauty. Moreover, here I really don't have words to explain how she took my heart or about her beauty"

"I would like to see my hero's choice. Do you have some photograph of her? I am sure, you must have one.", asked the sister intervening.

"For sure dear, you have all the rights!" acknowledged Vivek.

"And where I can find her picture dear?"

"If you really want to see, then it is there at my home, in my cupboard, beneath the newspaper. I used to put my books on it. But, there is a request sis."

"What?"

"Please do not share it with my sister Drishti, as she would feel awkward, knowing this now."

"Okay, I will not do anything you don't want me to do."

Drishti was listening to all this, she entered the room after half an hour, in order to hide the truth, she had come to know.

"Brother, I need your help", asked Drishti entering into his room.

"Yes tell me sis."

"See, I am a bit confused. I have a little work in Siddhartha's office. So, should I leave this document here? And if you could please ask him to get it done for me? Or I should get it done myself?"

"And what you are going to do now, otherwise?"

"I will go to home straight, take some rest and will come back with your food."

"And where is Siddhartha's office?"

"On the way."

"So? Why do you want to bother him for this small work, dear? He comes here after working for eight hours and then I give him another work. This would not be right at all. I request you to go to his office and get it done today. Please!"

"Okay, Okay. I will do that. You don't take tension about your friend. Ok!"

That evening, when Siddhartha came to meet him, Vivek was about to tell him about his pain. On the opposite Siddhartha, holding his hand, jumped in joy as he was excited to share something with him. Vivek kept himself low and calm and was now eager to know the reason behind his joy. In a couple of seconds, when Siddhartha was jumping, many thoughts came to his mind like—his first promotion or perhaps he has got a new job with higher salary, or one of his dreams of becoming an entrepreneur was going to be accomplished soon and so on. However, all these became meaningless, when he told him the exact reason. it was the one, for which Vivek was waiting for actually. He told him that he was in love now and it did not happen suddenly. He was now above the sky and feeling great about himself and his present situation. He was excited and thrilled and it was clear from his face that he was happier and enjoying that moment, even more than Vivek could see. This happens only once in somebody's life that he/she is ready to give his/her time to someone else, when thinking about her/him or brewing new ideas to impress her/him. You are ready to give everything you have, to make someone happy or set an impression of quality in somebody's eyes. The weather was becoming more charming, as well as the day-dreaming was playing its role in his eyes with the breeze giving him a great confidence and internal excitement, which could let him do anything, and it was increasing in him. He was looking restless. His excitement was obvious as he was experiencing the most thrilling feeling on this earth–the love!

6

THE DEDICATION

Vivek forgot everything as soon as he heard the word, most important in his life, from Siddhartha and his involvement in the meaning of the word. Siddhartha and Drishti knew that Vivek was a big emotional fool and would easily get carried away, after hearing about it.

That day, Vivek's sister Drishti went to Siddhartha's office for her work, as he compelled her to.

"Hey! Brother", she said to Siddhartha while he was walking away in hurry.

"Hi! Sis, you here?" Siddhartha asked out of surprise.

"Yes! Got some work for you, Forgot?".

"Oh! I am sorry! I remember. Why did you bother, I would have taken it from Vivek."

"Well, actually I was also thinking of the same, but you know Vivek. He asked me to drop it here instead. So, here I am."

"Ok. Just give me one moment, let me ask where it will be done or which department it is related to?"

"You know that our offices are related to each other in legal field only. These documents have been sent to your office thrice now, but see, it is still incomplete because of your Accounts team."

"Oh! I am sorry about it. Just wait for a moment. Let me get it done for you."

"Don't worry. Just let me know, where to go. I will get it done myself now."

After confirming, he told her to visit the second floor of his office and take a left to meet someone named Laxmi.

Drishti heard the name and suddenly went into a flashback-"Laxmi! Vivek also said that he loves someone named Laxmi. What a coincidence!"

"Bye for now. Let me finish my work and I will inform you" said Drishti as she left.

"See you, sis. In case there is some problem, do let me know," replied Siddhartha.

"Sure brother"

Vivek's sister looked extremely happy, when she came out of Siddhartha's office. She called Siddhartha to say Thanks.

"Hey! dear bro, I wish she was the same Laxmi, my brother loved."

"What? You know about Vivek's romantic story and that girl? Is she the same Laxmi?"

"I heard about it today only, when he was talking to the nurse. I am telling you, this girl was just amazing. She handled my problem as her own and it was such a pleasure for my eyes to see a beauty like her with such a wonderful heart."

"Is it? Then I will have to meet her as well", Siddhartha was kidding.

"Okay Brother. Thanks a lot for the help today and hopefully, we will meet in the hospital for further talks about Laxmi", she smiled as well.

"Sure but no thanks sis, bye for now."

Vivek's sister reached home and sat on the sofa with a relaxing feeling. She took a deep breath and moving her neck in right direction, fixed her sight on some object. *This happens sometimes, that we do not have anything to think and we keep looking at some unknown point, on some object like wall, some picture on the wall or the doors.* Then, she thought, "What a wonderful day!" moved her neck in other direction and suddenly she gave a second thought to what she was looking at.

"It's Vivek's cupboard. Oh! Laxmi's photograph. Let me find it and see, who is she to rule my brother's mind and soul?"

She rushed towards the cupboard as if she was never tired, to find the photograph. After a bit of mess, she saw the back of the photo, which was pasted on the newspaper below the books, as she read the statement written on it.

"*My definition you complete, my existence you compete You exist here for me.*

You wrote one word–LOVE—to say it all, on, my blank sheet of my mind and soul.

You are my part and I am yours,

If I cheat you, actually whom do I cheat? I cheat myself.

In addition, when she turned over the picture, she was shocked.

She was the same Laxmi; she met in Siddhartha's office that afternoon. She was amazed and surprised at his brother's feelings.

"What do you write? What do you think bro? All your feelings create a new world and include us all. I came to know about this photograph, then you compelled me to go to Siddhartha's office and then I met the same girl, whom you loved. It is a miracle, complete miracle. I mean...How in this world is it possible. I need to inform Siddhartha about it."

This was a great coincidence though. Nobody had seen Laxmi before, even in the photograph. However, they had heard about her from Vivek only. It was Drishti only to know about Laxmi and meet her the same day, without Vivek knowing about it. That evening, Drishti told everything about it to Siddhartha and requested him to help her with her *plan*.

"Siddhartha, listen carefully. I feel that my brother's feelings are going waste like this. We really have to help his feelings reach Laxmi. You have to talk to her about it."

"How would I sis? It's not that easy. I even don't know her. I have never even interacted with her, and what we are going to tell Vivek about it?"

"Don't worry, I have a plan for that as well. How you will start and accomplish this."

Siddhartha along with Vivek's sister jotted down a plan to extract the love from Vivek, by creating a virtual story, in which they decided that they would tell Vivek that someone was there in Siddharthas office named Zubaan. And that Siddhartha liked her. All this was to be explained to Vivek, hiding the truth and in a virtual manner getting ideas from him, which actually were to be conveyed to Laxmi, as his original thoughts and feelings about her. They thought that if there is something called love, on this earth, it could happen like that as well, means, Vivek through Siddhartha loves Laxmi. The love extracted from Vivek, as if they were for Siddhartha, but to be conveyed to Laxmi as Vivek's own. They also decided that they would tell the situation of Vivek to Laxmi, only if the idea clicked and she would get impressed from his thoughts and love. That would be the real test of the purity of love as well.

7

THE BEGINNING

Vivek's help was required in that case because Love is an emotional thing, which can even make a lazy person do all the work alone and also much faster than anyone else and Vivek was a lover. Emotions are required in a work, if you want to win somebody's heart.

"So, are you ready to help me bro?" asked Siddhartha.

Vivek did not respond and looked in the other direction, as if asking the same question to God, "Will you help me, help him?"

"Vivek, I am asking you something dear!"

Vivek turned his face to him slowly. After looking at him for a while with a smile said peacefully, "I will give my soul for you dear. No question in it. Just let me know when you will tell about her to me? How she looks, how she talks, how you feel when you look at her?"

"Well, was it a single question? Ha...just kidding. I already told you that she looks beautiful. How she talks? I really don't know as we have not interacted yet. I feel in heavens whenever she is in front of my eyes."

"And what if she is not present?" asked Vivek intervaning.

"I feel sad as I feel like looking at her all the time and when she is not around, a strong desire pushes me to search for her."

"I think it is mere attraction brother. I am sorry, if I am rude but from your emotions, it doesn't look as you are in love. It is mere attraction only. Infatuation."

Siddhartha felt that it was getting difficult for him to answer to further questions from Vivek as he was instructed by Vivek's sister, they were not his original feelings. Now he was afraid that Vivek will soon catch his lie, so gave an excuse of an important phone call and came out of the room saying, "I am surprised that you don't understand these feelings. Just give me one moment, I need to make an important call."

Vivek smiled at his frustration and said, ok.

He was then talking to the sister.

"You know sister, he is still immature. His answers felt to me as if, he learned them somewhere. He has to feel the love before he expresses it."

"Well, I really don't understand then what love actually is and how to feel it like you. Take these medicines and let me go and get some tea for you both. Love love love. You too grow up and do something other than love now. Only one thing always", said the sister picking up the used utensils from under Vivek's table.

"Is everyone frustrated? Okay! I will say nothing about love anymore. I think you all have understood it completely now."

"That is not the reason at all. You keep telling people about love and yourself, you did not express even and still are not trying", the sister expressed her point.

Vivek taking a deep breath said, "I know you are right, but..."

"What?"

"I am a coward, otherwise, I would have expressed at that time only. And I know it is too late! But I still believe that she is mine and with me always", Vivek looked very cute, when he said that. Thinking for a while he said, "Leave it. Let us have some coffee rather than tea. Let us make this hospital a small cafe." He was trying to change the atmosphere.

"Why not! I'll just come," and she left the room.

Siddhartha was outside talking to Vivek's sister Drishti, "Sis, it is too difficult for me to answer his little but dangerous questions. I am not a love freak. You know that. I cannot withstand this lie. I think I should tell him the truth that the girl is but Laxmi and we want to express his feelings to her."

"Please don't create that blunder. It will not be any fun then, thinking this story and playing these roles. You are doing right. This is going in the right direction. This is the way to bring his true feelings of love out and display them raw to Laxmi. It is good that you answer his questions incorrectly or insufficient. Just have some patience bro. Just for the sake of your friend only. Please...", said Drishti.

"But sis, I go numb when he asks something. Either you tell me what to say or it would be impossible for me. Try to understand!"

"I do, dear and I am there to help you with it."

"Okay. But how do you know what to answer?" asked Siddhartha.

"It's in the genes dear," giggled. "I know my brother very well and really respect his silent feelings."

"Alright! Now please tell me how to start again?", urged Siddhartha.

"Just listen to his questions and answer them in the most natural way, for it is good that you answer them wrong. But when he says something, listen carefully as these feelings will help Laxmi understand his true feelings and arouse her feelings for him as well."

"Let me see how I can do it. Though it really becomes difficult the first day itself", said Siddhartha taking a deep breath.

"My blessings are with you. Let true feelings be allowed to show their power. Ok bro, see you tomorrow."

"Yeah, that is good that you leave a nursery class student in tenth standard and still ask him to learn everything and answer all difficult questions as well. Alright! I will try to come out as a meritorious student here as well. Take care Sis. Bye now."

Siddhartha then went back to Vivek's room to face the challenge, the challenge to show love and learn it that way.

"Hey! I am back. Ask what you were asking at that time. Sorry, I had an important call", said Siddhartha putting his mobile in his pocket and entering the room.

"Nothing dear. I just wanted to learn love your way. As they say, there are various ways to express the same thing", said Vivek changing the flow.

"You will learn from me and that too love! Have you gone nuts? Are you crazy? I don't know L of love", Siddhartha said.

"Oh! Is it? Then who said I am in love? See dear, I really request you, not to create joke out of my feelings. This word itself gives me chills. My mind, my soul, my heart, my eyes and my ears, they all come at the same level at the same moment, when I hear about it. So, tell me if there is any girl in your office you like or is it just to play with my feelings?", said Vivek in a requesting way.

"There is...and she is very beautiful and I want to make her mine as well, dear. I need your help for the same, as I really don't have those dense feelings yet, which you have been feeding inside you for last seven years. You have experimented with them so many times, that only you could understand the power of love", said Siddhartha emotionally, as he knew that Vivek was an emotional guy and this was surely going to help.

The sister entered in the room and said, "Coffeeeeee. Let's make it large."

"But I never talked to any girl in my life like that, you already know. Then why do you think, that my feelings can help you?"

There was complete silence in the room, as Siddhartha had no answer to his question. Suddenly, the sister stepped in and answered to his question on behalf of Siddhartha.

"You know something, dear. The words you say filled with the great thoughts and feelings show your experience itself. If they ignite us then they can ignite anyone in this world."

"You tell me, if you are willing to help me or not? Or you will just keep proving your worth for us?", said Siddhartha teasing him.

Vivek said, "It's Okay! Don't worry. I will surely tell you what to do. Let us enjoy the sweet coffee, sister has prepared with heart for us. The only thing, you need to do tomorrow is to look at her carefully and understand her beauty from a distance, hiding yourself from her eyes. We will come to them afterwards. Let me know how she looks—her facial expressions and feature like eyes, nose, eyebrows, lips, most important her hair. You fall in love with them forever you know, apart from the love from soul. Right?"

Siddhartha said, "for sure" and finished his coffee and left the ward.

Siddhartha called Drishti before starting his car."Hey sis! He made it easy for me somehow. God really saved me tonight. I hope it will be better tomorrow as well!"

"I believe everything will be alright. Now, you have to start interacting with Laxmi as well. Go ahead. Tell her the truth tomorrow anyhow", Drishti pushed him.

"Oh my God! Is Vivek not enough to handle that I will have to talk to Laxmi as well?"

"See bro, try to understand, you have to do it and believe me, it's easier to tell the truth to Laxmi rather than handling Vivek. At one place you have to grab the true feelings and at the other place you need to express them as it is. I know it is a bit hard for you, as you don't understand these feelings right now, but you will understand them one day and pat your back for you did it. Just help me for some time in this bro, I will never ask for more from you. Please..."

"Sis, you never have to say that word to me. It is only, I have never done anything like that. But I promise, I will try my best. But at least tell me how I will recognise her?"

"Oh Yes! I forgot to show you that magical photograph. Where are you? I have that photo with me. I will show it to you", said Drishti.

"That is brilliant. I am in the hospital parking. I will wait for you here. Come soon."

Drishti's strong desire to help his brother also moved the

'not so confident' Siddhartha to help her in her kind mission. Drishti got the lift and went to the hospital parking to show him the photograph of Laxmi, so that he could recognise her easily.

"Dear I am sorry to keep you waiting", said Drishti.

"No worries sis, let me see my sister-in-law quickly. Even I am excited to see that beauty."

Drishti pulled the photograph from her purse carefully.

"See, how cute and beautiful she is and read these magical words from your brother on its back", said Drishti, as if very proud of her brother's choice.

Siddhartha read the fourlines and looked at Laxmi's photograph, said, "Oh my God! She really is a divine beauty. Now I understand, why Vivek is such a brilliant lover."

"I think, now you will recognise her easily. Now Good Night, it is already too late"

"Anyone can recognise such a unique beauty. I will update you tomorrow then. Good Night!"

The next morning, as soon as Siddhartha reached his office and was thinking about how he will start interacting with Laxmi, his boss entered his cabin and said, "Hey Siddhartha, I have decided some changes for you. Just report to me quickly in my office."

Siddhartha was a sincere employee and followed his boss's command ever instantly. He picked his notepad and pen, and knocked his boss's door, "Sir, May I come in?"

"Yes. Please have a seat. See Siddhartha, we have grabbed this new opportunity and I think that only you can handle these new and important projects. Have a look", said his boss putting the project file on the table.

Siddhartha read the project file briefly and said, "It surely is a great project, Sir and I thank you for your confidence in me."

"But the client wants you to work at his place for it. Are you ready to move to his place at Bangalore?", asked the boss.

Now, it was a bit difficult for Siddhartha to answer, as he was thinking something else, but had happened something opposite. He was thinking about the same.

"What happened? Are you not ready?" asked the boss again.

"No Sir. That is not the case", replied Siddhartha still thinking.

"Then get ready for your flight day after tomorrow. Take this file along. They do have their office here as well, but they want us to work at their Bangalore office. Don't know why? I hope it is fine for you day after tomorrow, or tell me by night, if you need some time. Right?"

"Yes sir!", said Siddhartha and picking up the file came out of his boss's room.

He was unhappy now as he won't be able to help his friend get his love.

As he sat on his chair, his mobile had ring.

'Vivek-Hospital', read the phone screen.

Negative thoughts came in his mind about happening something bad happening to Vivek, as this was the number the sister used to call for asking something for Vivek. However, today as his mind was in an opposite state, he could not think positively.

He picked up the call and it was Vivek on the other side.

"Vivek! Is it you? Are you alright? What happened?", a flood of questions from Siddhartha sprang.

"Oh! I am absolutely fine. Sister is here with me. She is holding the phone on my ears. I can hear and speak. Listen! I was thinking why do not you talk to her today itself?"

"Who?" asked Siddhartha forgetting that he was a part of an important play.

"Oh my God! I am talking about the girl in your office. See, again you will say, I don't understand your feelings. But I think you are not serious at all. See sister, he is asking which girl!"

"Oh! Actually I was a bit tensed today dear. I was thinking about something else", said Siddhartha rubbing his forehead and relaxing on his office chair.

Vivek was a bit tensed now as was clear from his changed tone of the voice.

"What happened dear? Please tell me. I am a bit worried now!", expressed Vivek.

"Nothing, dear. I have been transferred to Bangalore from tomorrow", said Siddhartha.

"Oh! That's sad really. But I think everything happens for good. Perhaps due to this emergent situation, you will be encouraged to talk to her before leaving!"

Vivek was still positive and wanted to turn the situation as an opportunity for Siddhartha.

"Are you mad, dear? She doesn't even know me. How can I talk to her like that? Does it make sense at all?", said a bit frustrated Siddhartha.

Vivek did not answer straight away and after thinking about the situation for a while, said, "No, I don't think it is weird. And I think it is possible, but if you yourself don't want to do it today, it is a different case. But, I will pray hard to the Almighty that somehow you both should talk today. And about your transfer, let's see if there is some solution", said Vivek with a soulful prayer to the Almighty.

"Ok dear, I will see you at the hospital tonight then", said Siddhartha and ended the call.

He thought for a while and a thought came in his mind to share the situation with Drishti. He called her immediately.

"Hey sis, everything got messed up today. I have been transferred to Bangalore from tomorrow and your romantic brother is asking me to talk to Laxmi today at any cost. He is crazy. He never did it himself and thinks that others can do it so easily. What should I talk to her? tell!"

"Calm down dear. Firstly, it's sad news. It has ruined our plan and also you and Vivek will not be able to meet daily now. I know it is difficult but Let's think positive. Perhaps this is the way God has created for you to take control of the situation and tell her about Vivek before you leave for Bangalore! Do you?"

"Both of you are same. He was praying to God to make us talk today and you also want the same now."

Suddenly, the office boy came in Siddhartha's cabin and told him that boss had called him.

"Ok sis, I will talk to you later. Boss has called me. See you."

Siddhartha put the phone down and taking the project file along, went straight to his boss's room.

He knocked on the doors, opened and asked, "Sir, may I...?"

"Yes...yes. Come in", intervaned the boss.

He entered the room, closing the door silently. He saw a girl standing in front of his boss's desk from behind. He was active now.

"Yes sir."

"Siddhartha, meet Ms. Laxmi, she will assist you and will move to Bangalore along with you."

The girl looked back at Siddhartha as the Boss was introducing her to him.

"Laxmi works in Accounts on the second floor", Boss continued.

Siddhartha looked up at once and was immensely shocked to see her. He could recognise her easily and was thinking of Vivek's prayer in a moment of silence.

"What happened? You know her?" asked the boss after he saw Siddhartha looking constantly at Laxmi.

"Yes! I mean No sir! Hello", replied a stunned Siddhartha in greeting to Laxmi.

"Hi!" She said.

Now, the boss was talking again.

"She will assist you and you have to help her reach Bangalore and get a good and safe place there as well. As you are the senior, so I want you to work the things accordingly. You may go now and talk to each other and the people in Bangalore to arrange your stay and work there."

"Ok sir. Thank you! Come to my cabin Laxmi. It is third cabin as you take a right", Siddhartha came out of the boss's room along with Laxmi.

He looked up amazed and was talking to God, "You really listen to him now? Oh Man! I denied talking to her and now we will work together. Ha...Amazing. Simply amazing! She really is a pious beauty."

Laxmi came to his cabin and stood there until he requested her to sit, "Please have a seat dear. Relax and feel easy. You want to have some coffee or tea or some soft drink?", asked excited Siddhartha.

"No sir. It is fine. I just have a request, please", said Laxmi.

"Sure, tell me!"

"Sir, it is very difficult for me to shift to Bangalore as I am the only caretaker of my old mother. My father is in Police and gets transferred often. Also, she has spent her life time here. She has all her friends and a few relatives here. I hope you understand!" said Laxmi with a sad face.

Siddhartha didn't understand, as he was not that emotional and said, "What can I say dear. It is the office that has decided and we need to follow as it is."

"But...Sir!" Laxmi was about to say something but Siddhartha interrupted, "Let's wait and see if something can be done. Let's exchange our numbers, so that we can communicate."

They shared their numbers and Siddhartha said, "Alright now. Take this file, read it to get an overview about what we need to do there. Anything else? Feel free to say."

Laxmi replied, "No sir, it is fine" and went out disappointed.

As soon as she went out, Siddhartha called Drishti to express that amazing moment to her.

"You won't believe what happened just a few moments ago. My God! I never believed that prayers are heard like this also. Sis, your brother is a magician of feelings."

"Don't tell me you met her", said an overwhelmed Drishti.

"Yeah..."

"Really! But how?" now Drishti was over excited to know everything about it.

"That wave of thrill, when she looked at me. Oh! The wave was so heavy, as it passed through my heart as if I felt God in form of an eye contact with my sister-in-law. You know Sis, only a few moments before, Vivek said that if I don't try to talk to her today, then he will pray that it should happen somehow and see, how interestingly our boss introduced us. I mean it's unbelievable for me, really! And now I have even her contact number. Oh my God...you are there. I saw you today through her. You are there through my friend as well. You have blessed him with the power of love and wait. Sis, I am really happy for Vivek today and being a part of his amazing virtual love story."

Drishti smiling and with unstoppable tears in her eyes said proudly, "I knew my brother has some powerful feelings in his heart. I knew that..."

"Hey sis, no need to cry. You should be happy that a person who asks God for us to play his story is so close to us."

"I am happy, dear. Actually amazed and happy, even when I know that God does it all, but how He gives us different roles is something that we will never understand."

"But there is one problem Sis", Siddhartha said.

"And what is that, dear?"

"You know why our boss introduced her to me?"

"Why? Yes, I forgot to ask this in excitement actually."

"Transferred to Bangalore, she will assist me there, in finance and accounts. But, she doesn't want to go there due to her ailing mother."

"Perhaps there is some reason for that. Let us tell Vivek, in accordance with the story and seek help from him. So, before we enter his room tonight, we will decide first, what and how to tell him, and how to get an answer for this query as well. Ok? Bye for now! See you soon, dear".

"Bye sis, I will reach there early today around 5:30".

That evening, Drishti and Siddhartha met at the hospital reception before they saw Vivek.

"See there is a plan, it's actually not a plan. We will try it this way—You will tell him that it is your boss who introduced you both for the project you will work on and that she will assist you there, but she doesn't want to go to Bangalore. Let us see, what he suggests then."

"Alright, as you suggest sis. You are the teacher, I am the student. I will follow as you instruct. You know that, I can't mould things especially where feelings are involved", said Siddhartha.

"And remember one important thing!"

"What?"

"He will ask her name dear, so what name should we give to Laxmi?"

"Let it be Laxmi only, when everything will be explained to him as it is. Is n't it?", inexperienced Siddhartha said.

"Oh my God! You are...completely off. Tell him that she is Laxmi! So that he understands everything in first go. You know that he calculates, whatever he listens. Leave it. We will call her "Zubaan", and tell him that she is a Muslim girl. Give that Romeo some spicy challenge. This way, we will also know his real thoughts on inter-religion marriage as well as exact definition of love for him", explained Drishti.

"Hmm...Interesting", accepted Siddhartha.

"But this will make things difficult for me, sis", said a bit worried Siddhartha.

"I know that. But then, I am there to help you at every step. Remember always, we are creating this story for the sake of true feelings. So let us try our best, and rest let it be as Vivek says, 'This is he through us'. Believe me, it will be a successful attempt, only we don't have to give up", said a positive Drishti.

"But we have been transferred to Bangalore, sis. How we will continue then?", interrupted Siddhartha.

"Don't worry, dear. I firmly believe now that God will help somehow. Let us move in now. You go first and I will come after half-an-hour at least, to avoid his intution catch my involvement anyhow. Go for it. You can do it."

"Thanks Sis. I really need those wishes. See you."

Siddhartha went inside Vivek's ward, where he and Nurse Sister were interacting.

"Hey! Here he is. We were waiting for you eagerly. So, Mr. Professional will be shifting tomorrow to the Silicon City!", said Vivek welcoming Siddhartha.

"What Silicon City dear. It is not way big for me", said a disappointed Siddhartha.

"Why dear? It was your dream to be there someday as a representative of some MNC and you got this chance straight within only two months. I am happy for you, dear".

"Yeah that is...but you know, who is assisting me there?"

"Who?" interrupted the sister.

"Who dear?" urged Vivek.

"Guess who?" Siddhartha tried to increase his excitement further.

Vivek looked at him with a smiling face and teasingly asked, "Hmm... That girl?"

"How do you know? sister... How in this world he already knows this? Who told him about this?" Siddhartha made a crying facial expression.

"All my surprises vanished. Ann... That is not fair!" he continued.

"Hey dear relax. I just guessed it and first of all, I am very happy, that I guessed so. But I mean really? She will assist you there? Oh my goodness. Then everything is so simple for you now. God bless you, dear", said a very happy Vivek.

"But there is a problem, dear friend", interrupted Siddhartha.

"I knew that. But don't worry. There must be some solution as well. Before everything else tell me, what is her name and how is her voice?" excited Vivek asked.

"Well her name is Zubaan and her voice? What her voice?", asked a confused Siddhartha.

"Obviously you would have talked to her or you must have heard her voice. So, what was it like? And name, you said Zubaan. Is she a Muslim girl?" asked Vivek with his eyebrows raised.

"Yes, she is. What do you want to say now?" answered Siddhartha trying to test his opinion on the same.

"I liked it. It is going to be more interesting now! So, she meets, she will assist you and you will have all the time to spend together and she is a Muslim girl as well. Is it all planned by God, and he wants the purest form of love to be implemented here, as you have a challenge to show people, that we are here to create love, not religions. Hmm...Interesting. Love prevails where the situation is not supporting. What is the problem now?"

"She doesn't want to go there, due to her ailing mother", told Siddhartha.

"Then that's a solution, not a problem dear", said Vivek with a smile.

"How?"

"My dear brother, when she doesn't want to go, and you are her boss , the law would says, you should fight for her right to stay here", explained Vivek.

"Ha...How can you be so positive? How is that possible when boss of her boss has ordered the same?"

"Request! Request is the word as per the current situation and I firmly believe in the power behind this word. You need to talk to the humble side of your boss and tell him the truth about her mother and wait...there must be another solution as well, man. This is not the first problem on this earth without a solution."

Vivek as usual thought about it from a different angle with typical problem resolving tendency rather than confusing over the problem.

Now, Siddhartha also gave it a second thought.

"Yeah! Actually you are right. There is a solution. Our clients do have their office in Delhi. But how would I ask my boss about it. No, that won't work", Siddhartha gave a solution and denied it at the same time.

"Excuse me dear. You love her, right?", said a bit amazed Vivek.

"Yes I do, but that doesn't mean I play with my job for her small wish. Its only two months since I have joined the company and it is the first project, I have been assigned and you want that I should deny working on it?" said Siddharth, a bit worried.

"I want! No! It is what you want!", said Vivek silently.

"Why should I want it? Please tell me!"

"She wants it. That is , you have to try to get the same done for her. You have to try, and that doesn't mean the end of your job. If you can't try this even for her, then forget her friendship dear. It is not love. It is not attraction even", Vivek was not happy at all. He was disappointed and was looking up constantly without a single word.

Entered Drishti and looked at both of them in a silence, and asked Vivek, "Everything right here? What happened to you? Why are you looking at that fan, as if it will start all of a sudden after a few moments? Hmm...?"

"Nothing sis. We were just thinking that whether I should join his company or open our own, when I get well", Vivek tried to hide the fact that he and Siddhartha were talking about love, as it would have been awkward for him to talk on such topic with his elder sister.

"Ok, if you don't want to share then it is fine. I just wanted to take your medical slip to bring your medicine. Also, I had to tell that Rahul (their cousin) would stay here tonight, in case you need any help", saying this she went out from there.

Meanwhile, Vivek realised that Siddhartha was not so romantic or understanding person, therefore he politely started requesting him, "See dear. Please try to understand. If she wants to stay here only, then you should try on her behalf, as she being shy, will never say anything but, at least you should understand. Kindly try at least once for me!"

"See professionally, it is not good at all to ask for any personal favour. But as you say, I will at least try my best. Is it fine now? Happy?" said Siddhartha.

"Yeah! More than happy. At least, I get one thing for tomorrow to do", said Vivek smiling.

"What is that?" asked Siddhartha curiously.

"I can pray for both of you and her wish to come true. What else can I do now? But, please try, ok!" said an emotional Vivek.

"Yeah! I will. She is I, and I am she now. Right Mr. virtual lover?"

"Thanks buddy. But still, you did not tell me, how her facial features look like?"

"I will explain, but I need to understand myself first. Good Night. Need to read that Bangalore file as well", said Siddhartha moving out of the ward.

"You both will stay here only. Prayers will be heard, for they will take some time, I know I have to wait till then. At least we should register our request dear. Take care of her smallest wish. That is the way to help create a bond that will last forever."

"Will try. Bye now".

Vivek had so much to say to arouse feelings in Siddharth, but restricted himself and healed his heart telling himself, "He has just started. A long journey to travel. Calm down Vivek. At last love will surely pay all debts."

As Siddhartha came out, he called Drishti again, "Sis, he says, I should request my boss to allow us to work here only. Now you tell me what to do?"

"He is right. Try the same tomorrow and tell me what your boss said. See, we all have to be at one place to execute the things. I am sorry, if I am getting selfish here. But please for our brother. I don't want him, to lose you and Laxmi like this. I request you to ask your boss for this personal favour. I won't compel you, as I can understand that it's an opportunity for you. Still you have enough time to pursue your dreams. Let us do it for him this time".

"I got it Sis. I am also not such selfish as I can't understand that I have to do it for my dear friend and I will do it tomorrow and try my level best. Good Night!"

Here Vivek had started working on the project "Stop transfer".

He was asking Sister to pray along with him for Zubaan.

"We both are idle. Let us pray for her wish to come true. I wish their boss himself change the plan. Some miracles can happen like that, you know. God please, for the sake of true feelings."

For whose wishes he was praying actually? His sister Drishti's feelings for her brother? Laxmi's feelings or his own? God is such a great organiser that he indulges everyone, if he wants anything to happen actually.

8

THE MEDITATION

Next morning, Siddhartha called Drishti asking, "Hey sis, at least tell me what I should ask my boss. Wait! I think my boss is coming this way. I'll talk to you later".

"Ok! Best wishes!" understood Drishti.

Siddhartha's boss entered his room with greetings and giving him a card said, "Hey Sid, this is Mr. Amar's card, the Project head for that project, I talked to you about. (Pause...) See, I want you to stay here only and help me in the current projects going on in the company. I want you to talk to him and arrange for yourself and Laxmi to work at their office here only. You understand?"

Siddhartha standing on his seat and holding the card said, "Yes, sir. I will surely do that".

"Yah sit down. Let me see, how you do it. Just impress him with your communication skills as you impressed me with your work, because I don't think that in today's time, when we have all the technologies, then we can't work from here for them. And do remember, we should not lose this project in the way. If required, you may go there once in a while. Ok, Best wishes."

"Thank you for the opportunity, sir. I will give my best to get it done, as you suggested. Even Laxmi wanted to stay here because of her mother's condition", said Siddhartha.

"So, you have two strong reasons to ask them for us to work from here for them. Take care and report to me about the proceedings. See you", said the boss and went out.

Now, Siddhartha was talking to himself, "I was thinking that how I will request boss and here he comes to me to get the same done, what I was going to request him about. Isn't it amazing? Let me talk to Mr. Amar. God bless me."

He called Mr. Amar and told him the truth, "Good Morning, sir, this is Siddhartha calling from Loyal Technologies Pvt. Ltd. We will be handling your project of developing Accounts software"

"Oh! Hi Siddhartha. It is great to hear from you. Yes, tell me", said Mr. Amar.

"Actually sir, I had a humble request for you!" *Siddhartha remembered what his friend told him about talking to the humble part of a person.*

"Sure tell me", said Mr. Amar, responding like a very responsive and responsible person altogether.

"Sir, if we could work from here on your project at your Delhi branch as my colleague is the only caretaker of her mother and also officially, we will have complimentary support from our whole team here as well. Just on the base of basic human behaviour, we really need this help from you Sir, without compromising the quality of the work, we will deliver", requested Siddhartha.

"Well dear Siddhartha, let me tell you something here. I understand being human; however, I will have to take the permission from our directors. Give me some time, so that I can discuss the matter with them, if this is the case. I'll call you tomorrow. Keep your fingers crossed till then. I can't assure but yes, I'll surely try", said Mr. Amar.

Siddhartha described his discussion with Mr. Amar to his boss. He appreciated him, "Good attempt. Let us see, what is their decision."

Siddhartha again explained the complex situation to Drishti.

"Don't worry. Everything will be fine. I believe in God", said a positive Drishti.

"That is fine, sis, but what should I say to Laxmi then?" asked Siddhartha.

"Tell her to relax as the request is with the management now, and give her positive vibes that everything will go right and that you will try your best to get it done. For the rest your brother must be praying as well, I know. His wishes won't go waste."

"I also feel the same, because Mr. Amar looked human. Let us pray for our brother. May his love win over adverse situations. Ok sis, see you then."

"Bye, dear. Thanks for the prayers."

"You made me feel different there. Can't I pray for him? I have learnt it only from him."

"No, that is not the case, dear. I take the thanks back. Ok!" Drishti tried to recover.

"It's ok sis, See you. I need to talk to Laxmi as well."

Siddhartha then went to Laxmi to tell her the new developments..

How a crazy workaholic person was moving for somebody's feelings to get some lofty *residue* was something amazing for a person like Siddhartha. That is the way God follows to help the feelings travel through each other and finally stay here on earth for ever.

"Thanks for your kindness, sir, for you are doing so much for me", said a highly obliged Laxmi to Siddharth, when he told her about what he was trying for.

"No, it's not me, Luxmi. It's my friend who taught me to be as I am. I shared your problem with him yesterday and he asked me to make the request for you. So, all thanks to him."

"Wow. Then thanks to that kind soul, sir."

"I'll surely forward your thanks to him. Still, we have to keep our fingers crossed as the final decision is pending", said Siddhartha.

"Yes Sir, I hope Mr. Amar will help us. Fingers crossed."

"I will update you about it. See you then", said Siddhartha moving back to his cabin.

Laxmi was really happy for Siddhartha's kind gesture and jumped in joy, as he left from there, "Thank you God. Thank you for providing me a chance to work with such a kind boss."

But who knows what is in store for someone? That night Siddhartha elaborated the whole developments to Vivek to get his thoughts on the same and also check his feelings.

"So, what do you think? Will Mr. Amar help us?" asked Siddhartha.

"There is a clear justification system of the Almighty and it applies to feelings as well. The intensity of your feeling decides its outcome. You cannot fight with God for injustices of any kind. His judiciary is clear, direct and already justified."

"What does that mean?" Siddhartha did not get a word out of what Vivek said.

"It means the result will be according to your efforts. The more you put in, the more you get out of it", explained Vivek.

"Still not clear. Kindly elaborate it further."

"Leave it, dear. You won't understand at present. Gradually, you will understand these things. Don't worry. Go with time. It will teach you all the things slowly", said Vivek.

"Ok, I'll just come. Need to talk to someone", Siddhartha went out in search of Drishti.

As he went out, he saw Drishti coming with two bags in her both hands, along with Vivek's mother.

"Sorry dear. I got a bit late. Had to buy these fruits for him, you know", said Drishti.

"It's fine, sis. Good evening, Aunty. How are you?" he greeted the mother.

"Good evening son. I am absolutely fine, just a bit worried for Vivek", said Vivek's mother with wet eyes.

"Hey mom. Not again. See how strong your son is and you...Go and meet him and shower as much love on him as you want", Drishti handed over the fruit bags to her mother and encouraged her.

"You both also come inside. I will cut these fruits also for you both", Vivek's mother opened the doors of Vivek's ward.

"Yeah, we will come in a moment", said Drishti pushed her mother gently inside.

"So, what happened, dear?" Drishti asked Siddhartha.

"Sis, I really don't know what your brother talks about

sometimes. Everything goes overhead. Really!", said Siddhartha with a confusion expression.

"I can understand, dear. You will understand these things after sometime. Believe me. Till then, tell me what Laxmi said after you told her the things?"

"She thanked your brother. She really is a nice girl."

"I know that, and that is why I want my brother's feelings to reach her soon. Any girl would cherish such a lover and admirer, as Vivek is for her. Let us wait for tomorrow and hope for the best."

"Ok sis. I would leave now. Need to do some work tonight. Talk to you tomorrow", Siddhartha was in a hurry.

"At least have some fruits. Mom must have cut them by now", Drishti tried to stop him.

"No Sis. Try to understand. I need to go. Good Night", Siddhartha left.

Vivek's mother and sister also went out after talking to him for about an hour, as it was around 10 pm. That night, his mother remained in the hospital and his sister went back home.

Next morning, around 10:30 am, Vivek asked sister to call Siddhartha to know what happened, what Mr. Amar said regarding their transfer.

"Hello Siddhartha, it's sister here. Actually Vivek was asking about updates", reminded sister on his behalf.

"Oh yes sister! Thanks for reminding me. I am to call Mr. Amar and ask him. for the decision and call you back", said Siddhartha and dialed Mr. Amar's number as soon as the call ended.

"Good Morning, sir. This is Siddhartha calling again. Sir, just wanted an update, if any", asked Siddhartha politely.

"Well dear. I tried my best but still the management wants at least you to come here initially to take all the inputs. However, for your colleague, there is good news. She may stay there as we can take up web conferences to explain the things required."

"Thank you so much for your kind effort on Laxmi's behalf, sir. So, when can I report to you?" asked Siddhartha.

"Day after tomorrow. I will arrange a meeting with you and the board of directors."

"Alright sir, let me update my boss about it and book my flight for tomorrow evening. Thank you again."

"It's fine Siddhartha. If you need some Hotel booking, kindly let me know well in time, I may arrange it for you in the company's guest house."

"Oh! That is so helpful of you, sir. Thank you for this help as well. If you could arrange it for me, that would be a great help. I will e-mail you personal details, if required."

"Sure. Just drop an e-mail about your programme now. I will revert once organised. I think you would need to stay here one night only. Once you know, what the company needs, you can work accordingly at our Delhi branch. So, you may return same evening. Book your flight accordingly", suggested Mr. Amar.

"Thank you so much for all the help, sir. You made all the things so easy for me. I will just send the e-mail, once I update boss about it."

"Ok, see you day after tomorrow. I will e-mail the information related to guest house as well to you."

"Thanks and bye, sir. See you."

Siddhartha then explained the situation as per the client's requirement to his boss, to which his boss told him, "You will represent the company there. I believe your talent and knowledge about the task to be accomplished. Go ahead and at least present them with company diaries each, as an official gesture from my side."

"Sure sir! I am really thankful to you for the confidence you have in me. I will give it all to take this company higher with my presentation there", acknowledged Siddhartha.

"Go, get it for all of us."

"Sure sir!", Siddhartha went to his cabin to drop an e-mail to Mr. Amar about his programme.

Mr. Amar also responded back soon, as required. Siddhartha got his flights booked accordingly and updated Drishti about the same.

"Sis, he said it right that prayers are heard. Laxmi will not go to Bangalore and I too have to go there once in a while, as decided after today's discussion with Mr. Amar. That means we will stay only here."

"That really is great news. Let us share it with the lover boy tonight."

"For sure, sis. It is all for him only".

"But according to the story dear. Beware".

"Yeah. You reminded me on time, or out of excitement, I would have shared it with him. Tomorrow, I need to go to Bangalore. Before that I need to update Laxmi about it, do some packing at home and will discuss many things with you tonight. See you."

"See you dear. Take care. See you."

That night both Siddhartha and Drishti decided. Siddhartha will tell Laxmi about Vivek as soon as he come back from Bangalore and he went back early from the hospital for some packing. Vivek wished him and told him something important, as a mentor.

"Dear, All your wishes have come true. Say thanks to Almighty for all that He arranged for you. Your boss said rightly, You will represent your company there. I don't doubt your capabilities, still I request you to stay earthed. Use your knowledge rather than excitement. to answer their queries. I am really happy for you and Zubaan. Even I will live a few more days in this happiness. Come soon and take care of yourself there", said a caring friend Vivek to an immature Siddhartha.

Siddhartha held his hand and said, "I will. Don't worry."

"And what are you going to bring for us from there?", asked Nurse Sister in between.

"Say, what you want dear sister?" said Siddhartha readily.

"Leave it, dear. I was just kidding. I know you won't be with much time there at all. Just come back with a successful project in your hands and make your ailing friend proud", said the sister.

"Yeah, I know that. But, if day after tomorrow, I get some time, I will bring some famous items from there. Ok, see you after two days. I will call you once I am free from the meeting there."

"No, just call when you land there. Good Night", said Vivek.

"OK, I will. Bye and take care."

"Wait...", said Vivek trying to get up silently.

"Now what?" said the sister, holding him behind.

"Keep Zubaan updated as well. That is important you know", reminded Vivek.

Siddhartha said smiling, "Sure" and thought, "How crazy he is in the name of love. He believes that there exists some girl named Zubaan and how hard he is trying to help me make a bond with her. Oh Lord! Please help me, help his true love reach Laxmi. It really is a tough task for me though", when he was leaving the Hospital that night.

Next day, Siddhartha called Laxmi in his cabin as his excitement did not allow him to wait further and said, "See Laxmi, there is a very important thing, I want to talk about."

"Sure sir!" replied Laxmi.

Suddenly Siddhartha's phone rang and it was Drishti calling him.

"Excuse me", said Siddhartha rising from his seat and moving out of his cabin.

"Sure sir", said Laxmi silently ready to wait for him after the call.

"Yes sis!"

"I called to tell you that just sow the seed inside Laxmi just before you leave. She may collect some energy to let it grow through the power from waiting."

"Means?"

"Don't tell her that there is one guy, who loves her so deeply. Just tell her that there is something very personal, you will tell her when you come back", explained Drishti.

"But why? I was just telling her about the same. What is the harm in telling her now sis?", said Siddhartha in a low tone.

"Talk to her about the project now in a very friendly manner. Build a relationship with her more frank and healthy, before sharing such a personal thing. Understand!" said Drishti with an authority.

"Ok, as you order My Lord!"

"Bye now and call me when you reach Bangalore!"

"Ok sis. Bye"

Siddhartha came back to his cabin, where Laxmi was waiting for him. Before he could sit on his seat, Laxmi asked," Yes sir, you wanted to say something!"

"Yeah! There is one thing, I wanted to tell you, but I will share it only when I come back from Bangalore. Meanwhile, you tell something about your family."

"It's a small family of four, sir. My father is in police who gets frequent transfers from one place to another. My mother remains ill most of the times, as she has some knee problem and younger brother is studying. But why are you asking all this, sir?" asked Laxmi politely.

"I told you there is something, I want to talk to you about. Wait till then. There is something, you must know. Have patience till then", said Siddhartha testing her curiosity.

Laxmi did not say anything after that and went from there, wishing Siddhartha luck for his mission.

This was a bit surprising for Siddhartha to understand her nature now.

'She is also a different person. He is also a different kind of person. I don't know what they think about normal things. Well, let us see after some time, what will happen with both of them. God, you have rightly put me between these confusing people', thought Siddhartha.

He had to take his flight at three afternoon, so he collected some previous documents from his boss related to client company and left for the airport.

This was his very first experience, so he was quite excited as well. While in the flight, he thought about Vivek and the story, he was a part of. The feelings were flying with him as well, as he was thinking about love there. He had many questions in his mind now. He wanted someone to answer to them at that time, but then looking out of the window, a thought came to his mind.

'What a life! No definition. How many roles do we play? How much do we try to make it sophisticated and how much it gets complex. How I changed from a dullard poor guy to a gentleman. Amazing!'

Then he thought about his friend.

'Vivek, a person who still remains the same, a passionate lover. An amazingly caring friend, a person who helped me change from an immature thin boy to a grown up, well built successful person with his positive attitude towards life and how he is today lying in a hospital with all his wishes and thoughts buried in his heart for rest of his life dependent on others to deliver even his messages. What is his destiny now?'

"Sir, are you looking for something?" Siddhartha heard the hostess asking him.

"No thanks. It's fine!"

He then thought again, 'Hey! Am I getting emotional here? Haah! Meet a changed Siddharth'.

"Excuse me!" he called the air hostess.

"Yes sir!"

"May I have today's newspaper please?"

"Sure sir!"

Rest of his time, went discovering something good for his profession.

The first thing he did, after landing to switch on phone and call to the Hospital.

"Hey sister! I have reached well here. Tell Vivek not to worry, Ok!"

"Great! Talk to him", sister held the phone on Vivek's ear.

"Hey! How was the experience, dear?"

"It was great. I will talk to you after my meeting is over tomorrow. I have to check first, where I need to go from here. Talk to you later", said Siddhartha in a hurry.

"Ok dear. Take care and best wishes for your meeting", said Vivek.

His meeting went great the next morning, as he was well prepared and had those nuts of encouragement from his friend, when they were in college. However, he couldn't get time to get something from there, as he had to collect the data from different people there. So, he went straight from his client's place to the airport, as he was getting late. When he landed at Delhi Airport, a thought again struck his mind, reminding of his dear friend Vivek.

'It is a bit strange. He is the only one, I would have called, today if he was fine. I have earned only one good person, so far. He said it right— 'It is how much efforts you put into a relationship and get the same back. Initially, one needs to give his/her all and gradually the other one learns to give at least something back. It is one's devotion towards building a relationship with someone, out of care or requirement and gradually they get indulged in each other's lives to the extent of helping each other. I wish he gets well soon".

These thoughts were taking him towards helping his friend in the way of communicating his feelings to his beloved. These thoughts were actually changing the way he used to think about love earlier as well.

As soon as he checked out of the airport, he called Drishti, Excited by thoughts— "Yes sis, I am back. Tell me now, how I should introduce Vivek to Laxmi?"

"Great! How was your trip dear?" asked Drishti.

"Trip was awesome! I am feeling more energetic, filled with enthusiasm and ready to work more. But, please tell me, how to talk to Laxmi now?"

"First of all, you don't have to introduce Vivek to Laxmi, it's his feelings for her, you need to express to her, in the same way they ignite us. Make her proud, that there is someone, who admires her to that limit and worships her as a Goddess. But let us meet tonight first and discuss", said Drishti.

"Sis, I am a bit tired today. I'll come only tomorrow evening. I am sorry about it", Siddhartha hired a taxi.

"That is when, you should do the things, when your body doesn't allow. I understand you are tired. Do one thing, come straight to the hospital and I will drop you tonight by my *scooty*", insisted Drishti.

"Ok, that's a good idea as well. See you sis."

He reached the hospital on time, where Vivek was waiting for him eagerly.

"Ok, the king is here. I welcome you back dear friend. How was it?" asked an excited Vivek.

"It was awesome. I came straight from the airport, you know", replied Siddhartha.

"What did the hostess look like?" asked an excited Vivek.

"You are asking this question? Strange!", said a surprised Siddhartha.

"It is the way you look at their beauty. They are ever charming and spread happiness around with their smiles."

"Well, they were beautiful that way. But, how do you justify looking at them, when you are already in love with someone?" asked Siddhartha.

"Hmm... Sit down first, you must be tired!"

"I will surely do that but only after you answer to my query!", Siddhartha was a bit disappointed with him now.

"To be loyal to your beloved and to love nature's creations do not conflict with each other, dear. I think you took it another way. I asked about the Air hostesses, which doesn't mean we can't admire their efforts, they put in to make the passengers feel easy and wonderful. I was a kid, when I went Chennai by air. At that time, I was much moved by their kind gesture. You know, I liked one of the air hostesses so much, that I asked her at least ten times to serve me water. I tried to learn how to greet someone, how to make someone happy with a smile, even when he is frustrated. I saw a sister in her and learnt these things. She was a natural creation, just like any other living being and they are blessed beauties. That doesn't mean, I wished to love her or it distracted me. It was just to learn the way how to admire things and appreciate them, as they are!" explained Vivek smiling.

"Then what about Laxmi? You loved her or are just attracted to her, as you were to an air hostess?" asked Siddhartha again.

"I love her. I still do and I will forever."

"But..."

"Yes, I am answering to your query only. See, to look at the air hostess and admire her natural beauty was a compulsion. But, it's the way you look at them. Are you trying to find your love in them or you will feel yourself lucky only, that you saw such a beauty! And I also don't remember now, how they looked. Coming back to Laxmi, she is here with me always. She is a soul thing. It is unique. I never felt any requirement to find anyone again, as I tried to search her. The waves, she generated in me were generated once and forever. The same was never repeated, even when I studied at a place like Chandigarh, the beauty hub. Her grace was with me always and her presence inside my heart, never allowed any kind of competition of her with any other beauty as well. It's just like—you see a beautiful face and pray to God to bless her beauty to be maintained for someone else, with a true heart. Why did you think that it can affect your loyalty?"

"I don't know. But it is fine now. I just asked because of the way you asked me about air hostesses"

"I never believed in the word—*Flirt*, It's love here, dear and not dirt! Ok let me elaborate further for your understanding. If you give a cow something to eat, she will show affections towards you. Love is there as well. She will even bless you. Animals do care about these feelings. World is the way you look at it sometimes, not the way it is. I might have elaborated it to you to justify myself, but I did it to help you revise your point of view. Any queries?", there was a piousness on his cute face.

Siddhartha was listening to him very carefully, as if he had to tell Laxmi, word by word.

"Nothing dear! It is clear now", replied Siddhartha.

"It's good that you have started asking questions about loyalty and love. It will help you understand your feelings better as well. Anyways, what is the plan for tomorrow?" asked Vivek.

"Hmm... Let us see, how it will help us. What sort of plan?" Siddhartha was a bit tired to understand his question exactly.

"How you will talk to her, for you both also will work on the same project? You will get to spend enough time with her, so you must understand the importance of this time you'll spend together", Vivek wanted him to focus now.

"Yeh! I understand that, but should I tell her about everything I feel at once?" asked Siddhartha.

"The way you can express your feelings is important. If your heart says that you are ready to express, go ahead, do it tomorrow itself. Or, wait for the time to fill those empty holes of understanding between you and her, then you can express your feelings. Choice is yours. Hear what your heart says and not what your mind asks you to do", Vivek preached to him.

"I am a bit tired tonight. Let me take some rest and decide with a cool mind and heart. I'll leave for the day. I hope you understand, dear", Siddhartha picked up his luggage.

"Sure dear. I can feel that you are tired. Go and take some rest, and start tomorrow with a smile on your face. You need to explain the things to her as what happened at Bangalore meeting. God bless you, dear. Good Night" said Vivek.

Siddhartha met Drishti outside and said to her silently, "I am going to tell her tomorrow for sure and trust me sis, I'll do it in the best way. I am sure she will understand."

"I trust you bro! Just do it. Let me know, if there is anything required". Drishti started her scooty.

She dropped him to his house that night.

"Good Night now".

"Good Night and Bye!", Drishti turned back to hospital to meet her brother and update him on the latest things going on in the family as well.

9

THE INTRODUCTION

The next morning, Siddhartha went to Laxmi and requested her for a meeting in his cabin after an hour. Meanwhile, he thought of the way through he would express his friend's feelings to her.

"May I come in sir?" a sweet voice entered his kingdom of thoughts suddenly.

It was Laxmi. He took a moment to look up to her.

"Yes please! Take a chair", responded Siddhartha.

Her simplicity was making it difficult for him to talk about Vivek. He looked in the opposite direction and asked—

"You would like to know which of the things first? Bangalore visit or the thing, I told you before leaving?"

"What was decided at the Bangalore meeting, sir? Did they allow us to work from here?" Laxmi asked eagerly.

It was a bit confusing for Siddhartha as he was expecting her to be excited about the personal talks.

He replied intelligently though.

"Well! Somebody prayed so worthy, that the directors of the company straight away allowed, which we wanted.,"

"Who prayed, sir?" now Laxmi was curious.

"This is what I wanted to share. I humbly request you to understand the things as they are, without taking it otherwise. There is one thing, you must know and believe. It was magic, how we met for somebody other's feelings."

"I really can't understand what you are talking about, sir. Whose feelings are you talking about?" interrupted Laxmi very politely.

"See Laxmi. It would feel to you as if it's an illusion, something untrue or magic. Kindly be patient to hear this. It's a true incident, I wanted to share with you. May I?", asked Siddhartha.

The time stopped for a while, when Laxmi was thinking on what to say, and Siddhartha was praying for her to understand, as he believed that he was not capable enough to express the feelings.

He again asked—"Please Laxmi, trust me! It is only for the sake of somebody's true feelings.

"Sure Sir. I will hear, but I hope it's nothing personal!" stressed Laxmi.

"You will understand it, once you listen to it carefully."

Laxmi was a bit nervous, as it was not normal for her to hear some incident like this, in which she was a part unknowingly.

Siddhartha started, "It started way back in 2005, when you were in Maa Saraswati School in eighth standard".

Laxmi was shocked to hear that and intervaned.

"How do you know, sir?"

"I'll tell you everything, dear colleague. Please be patient", requested Siddhartha.

There was complete silence in his cabin, as he continued.

"You used to come to the school on bicycle daily. There used to be your extra classes in the morning. You were a beautiful girl, busy with yourself and some friends, and there was a guy, very shy and afraid of you, who used to feel your beauty, hiding himself from you always."

"Sir, I am really afraid now. I really don't understand how you know all this. Were you the one?" asked Laxmi again.

"I am just a part of his story".

"Whose story are you talking about, sir? Please elaborate", said Laxmi.

"I am talking about my friend, dear. He is the one, who prayed for your wishes to come true, unknowingly. Still his feelings are so true that we both are sitting here, and not in Bangalore. You met his sister, a few days back. That was an outcome of his feelings as well. He was always afraid of your and never approached you with his feelings. He expressed his feelings to everyone he knew, but not you. I don't know whether he was afraid or it was destined as such only. He carried all those great feelings along with him, when he had to shift to Chandigarh because of his father's transfer. He never wanted to leave his native place though, as he was so attached to it and its memories. He didn't forget anything about you ever, as he used to fight with himself to keep the spirit of love alive in his heart forever. I met this guy around five years back and today even I am a changed man because of him, but he is still the same—A true lover. I never used to believe in his thoughts about power of love. However, he changed my thinking on the same as well, when I was dramatically introduced to you by our boss."

He continued, "Every moment I hear him say something about you, it seems to me, as if he has some magical power in his feelings. His words full of feelings in them, become so powerful, that his every prayer is heard in verbatius."

Laxmi was looking stunned at him, and he suddenly stopped.

He looked in the other direction and said again, "I think, you were right. We should not discuss these kind of things in our office hours. Let me tell you about the Bangalore meeting".

He felt as if everything he said went in vain. He respected his friend's feelings, and did not want them to go waste, without an effect. And this is what Laxmi replied to make it sure, "As you wish, sir"

That day, he did not say anything about Vivek and they both worked on the project work only.

This was a bit heartening for Siddharth, as he told Drishti about it,"Sis, there was no reaction at all. I mean that of strange. If somebody would have told me that someone loved me like that, I would have grown great and happy. I got frustrated there and stopped in lurk as I felt that all I said just went in vain. Was it right on her part, sis?"

"Hmm...I see. I think that was good indeed. She controlled her emotions. Girls often do that. Nonetheless, you calm down. It is a normal thing for girls and you did it right to stop in between. She must have questions in her mind now. Don't say anything now, until she asks. Right!". Drishti answered his query.

"Alright! As you say. But that was harsh, isn't it?"

"Everything will be fine, dear. You, too, have patience. Learn something from him, how he kept all those feelings with patience inside for seven long years", Drishti pointed her hand towards his sleeping brother.

Siddhartha looked at Vivek for a while and said,"He is amazing. I sometimes feel pity for him."

"Why to feel pity? He is not helpless. We are helping his feelings to get their reservors somehow, and I am sure, he would love to know this as well. This is what we are working for. Give me high-five for what we are trying."

That night Vivek was given some injection, so he had slept before his friend came to meet him that evening.

Next morning also, Siddhartha following his sister's advice called Laxmi for office work without talking about his friend at all. Though, he was praying for her to understand. Feelings were flowing and they were constant as well, building the effective surroundings.

Similarly, two days went without Laxmi asking about Vivek. Siddhartha was losing his patience now and approached his friend that evening and asked him.

"What if I express my feelings to her and she doesn't reply?"

"Ok! Listen carefully. She will reply for sure, if you express your true feelings. It depends on the weight you apply to your feelings. If she listens to you, that means something has been added from outside in her mind. She will calculate the things in her mind first. You need to wait till the words you said do reach her heart. She can take time for calculations."

"And what should I do till then?" asked Siddhartha.

"No hurry in love. It's a slow process. True love will take its time, but only to make its space in your beloved's heart for the rest of life."

"Yes! And then nothing happens. We have a live example with us—Vivek", Siddhartha took a hit on his friend.

"Don't take my example. I am still fighting with Him to justify my feelings for Laxmi".

"So, you think they were waste?"

"No! I strongly believe that He will justify them one day. Might be, after my death. Feelings were generated here inside me. I used media provided by Him to transfer them to Laxmi, but it has resulted without any visible effect so far. I am still trying. I believe some magic was there, it is still so there and will remain so forever. Feelings never go waste bro. They are a form of energy as per your science as well, they change their form only."

At this point, both Vivek and Siddhartha were thinking about the result of Vivek's feelings. Only their perspectives were different. Vivek was thinking that the book he was writing with the help of sister will help his feelings reach their destination finally whereas Siddhartha was thinking the other way. He and Drishti were following to transfer his feelings to his beloved Laxmi.

"I am still waiting for you to elaborate Zubaan's beauty. Let me see for how many days, I'll have to wait. I hope, I will be alive till then", said Vivek.

"I was just thinking about it only, how I am going to do that. I'll do it faster. I will not keep waiting like you", said Siddhartha immediately.

"Hmm... Then what does she look like? I am eager to hear that", said Vivek.

"Well... Let me imagine her in my mind, he pause". There she is. That beautiful face, when I looked at her for the first time", Siddhartha pretended hard on his memory and tried his best to elaborate Laxmi's beautiful face.

"Wait..." said Vivek.

"What?"

"One by one. say of her complexion first?"

"Pink. Yes, it's pink", Siddhartha had his eyes closed.

"Pink! Her face is pink in colour. Look carefully. It is pink or reddish?" asked Vivek creating an imaginative face in his mind.

"Yah! You said it right. It is a bit reddish", acknowledged Siddhartha.

"Look carefully! Her chin, is it small or broad?", asked Vivek again.

"It's somewhat, say, medium and with a cut at between. That looks beautiful actually!"

"Ok! Let us come to her lips, now"

"Upper lip, a perfectly M-shaped bow and the lower one makes it a weapon. Cherry-red, bright red lips. Wait...Yes... They are just perfect set of lips. I can remember them as it is. And they are cherry in colour with fine finishing lines", said Siddhartha concentrating harder on his imagination, trying to create her picture as if.

"Oh my God! You have observed her beauty so closely?" asked Vivek opening his eyes slowly.

"Don't disturb! It is really very difficult to describe someone like that. I am but trying to do that, and you should also imagine her, as I say", said Siddhartha concentrating more.

"Ok...Ok, moving on to the area above the upper lip, what does it look like?"

"Well...move up a bit. Her nose. I can't explain everything like that, even you understand this. And her nose is a small one, it's thin and with perfect tip. Looks great in its side view. It looks beautiful, you know".

"Now...wait... We are coming to the most important thing—her eyes, the gateway to her soul", interrupted Vivek.

"Yeah! They are magic. Big eyes, with rounded lashes. The first thing, anyone would notice. It's a bit hard to look into her eyes. They absorb the energy from you, if you look into them even for a while and this way they become more powerful. The way she keep them downwards and when you call her name, she will raise them up, only to confirm that they are more beautiful than you looked into them earlier. Her eyes are like that slow playing sitar, which you would like to listen more with every new tone. Her eyebrows are also naturally blended in such a perfect shape. Her forehead is clear and broad, white, and makes a perfect picture, in case you want to click".

"Her eyes are black or brown?" asked Vivek.

"Perfect black. Suits more on her face and makes it brighter as well. I mean, compliments her face, or I should say, her face compliments her oceanic dark black eyes."

Vivek turned into a flashback, as his imagination of Zubaan expressed by Siddhartha, helped him create a picture of his beloved Laxmi. But he did not say anything.

"It seems from the picture I could create in my mind, that she is a very beautiful girl and the way you expressed her beauty was something new as well, a bit scientific though. I am very happy for you dear and you said it rightly that beautiful eyes absorb the energy from your body. I remember that her eyes had washed all my sins!"

"Sins?" asked Siddhartha.

"Yeah! Sins. She purified my soul through her pious beauty and through the most beautiful things those eyes. It would become hard for me to sleep tonight, if I think more about her", answered Vivek closing his eyes slowly.

"What happened, dear?"

"I think I should die, now. It is becoming very difficult for me to carry these feelings in the desolate conditions, now"

"Please don't say that. How we would survive without you then?", said Siddhartha emotionally.

"I understand, dear. But sometimes, an empty mind takes me into flashback. I have tried a lot, not to think about her, but she captivates my mind anytime and...(Pause) Oh lord! Give me power to sustain life for the people who love me. Make me selfless!"

"But while you are thinking about her you are not thinking about yourself and thus you are selfless! Why do you think the other way?", Siddhartha supported him.

"There is no difference, dear...", said Vivek.

"How?"

"Ok! Let me ask you—Whom do you love the most? Think and tell", said Vivek.

After thinking for a while, Siddhartha answered, "I think myself."

"You are right! Everyone loves himself or herself the most. That is a natural thing. Even I do it. But now I am not in me. I find myself drowned in her. Her beauty is an ocean and I have been swimming in it since the day, I first saw her. Similarly, a mother finds herself in her child and loves him even more than her own body. As if a child is a part of his mother. Similarly, she is an energy source for me. I am a part of her this way and she is mine. Mother is an ocean for her child, as he looks up to her to feed him. She is an ocean for me as well. That is why I am not selfless, when I think about her. She is me, I am she. So, I love myself through her this way. She is my desire. But the aim is to be selfless, and I am still working on it. Understand dear?"

"Well, I can never think much deeply as you can. But tell me one thing, dear. If she is the energy which you survive, why don't you get her?"

"It is not to get her, it is to have her, dear. People want to get everything they love. But if I get the ocean in my control, I will get to know how to swim through it, which means the end of my journey. Why should I do that?"

"But this is not right. If you love someone, you must tell her. You are more selfish, if you don't do that. This way you are enjoying yourself without that person aware of it."

"You are right. This will happen, when both of us will have the same energy levels. At present, I am less powerful than her. It's not outwardbeauty's power only. I have to make my heart purified first, that if she wants to stay there, she would enjoy living there. That way, I will have some power to bring me identical and equal to her. Added to those if she has a beautiful heart as well, that will increase my work further. I will have to care more, love more and seek more from her. You will understand these things, when you will love Zubaan more. One day you will leave your ego behind and dedicate yourself to her. Listen to this song:

Listen my ego... Listen my ego!

When I will be in love...

You got to go!

I will not touch, I will not talk, and I will not feel anyone,

Until the work, of getting you, is done

So, listen my ego!

When I will be in love...

You got to go!

Some people, they tell a lie,

Truth when prevails, then why do they try?

Some people in love, still they shy,

Some people in love, still they cry,

But I'll not cry, I will not shy, I will not die anyhow,

Until I show, some day to you, how much I love you somehow,

For you are the one, I can give it all for

You are the one, before whoom, I will bow, so . . .

Listen my ego... Listen my ego!

When I will be in Love...

You got to go... You got to go!

"Hmm...Good song! Heard someone talking to his ego for the first time! But don't you think, these undelivered feelings somehow bother you ?", asked a curious Siddhartha.

"Let the love ruin me, let me die with a heavy heart, filled of undelivered feelings. I will cherish those moments forever when I was hit the very first time and was smiling, that was the time to realise that wait, patience, imagination and negligence are my friends and they will help me swim through this vast ocean of love unhurt, happy and satisfied without anything in hand, finally to meet my creator. You know pressure creates diamond, so does the heavy feelings of a heart", elaborated Vivek.

"Oh my Goodness lord! What a man you are! You are mad!"

"But I am happy", replied Vivek.

"Where did you learn all this from?"

"From within, from my natural instinct."

"But are you satisfied this way?" asked Siddhartha to clarify his doubts further.

"No! And I will never be. This is something I am learning and continue doing. That is why I say, I am fighting with God for this, but very politely. I am thinking, I am feeling and this way, I am expanding the reach of my feelings. Someday, they will reach her, I know".

"What if she gets married till then?", asked Siddhartha again.

"What change is it going to bring? What if she is married even now ?" said Vivek politely, pulsating with feelings.

"Well, why do you love her then? I don't understand at all", asked Siddhartha.

"She is an uncontrolled 'thought' in my mind and will stay there forever. I can't delete that thought. That thought gave me a lot of energy and has become a source for me. I did not love her; I was made to love her. I did not see her; I was made to see her. Similarly, I will never forget her; I will be made to forget her, perhaps by my death. Why I love her? I take it this way—to feed my soul with everlasting feelings and to intentionally give whatever I have to her through my dedication. Whenever, I saw her, she used to give me some energy in the form of attraction or those delicate feelings. Just like, a son looks for his mother to feed him, when he is hungry at birth and that attachment remains forever between them. Similarly, I used to look for her to generate feelings in me. Those feelings generated long ago, still remain here in me and that bond is strong enough to last till my last breath. That energy helped me play for my team and win the match as well, even when I was injured. I thought, she would look at me, at least once, when I will hit a goal. Though, it never happened actually, as I remember." He broke down. "Reason—She had more energy than me. She had the charm to make me happy, I didn't have. This acceptance made me a grounded person. The urge to make her mine, compelled me to work harder. Gradually, I absorbed energy from her and transferred that energy to everyone, I was in contact with. I needed energy, I used to look at her and then think about her. She changed a man into such a way as inspired him to love her more, to ask more from her indirectly, by thinking about her! She is the only magic, I learnt in my life. An indirect and indefinite source of energy available anytime and anywhere, emerging from within now. She is still so powerful, that I won't be able to dare talk to her and express."

"Then don't you want to associate her, now?"

"I wanted, when I was immature".

"And now?"

"I told you, dear. It was not to associate her, it was to have her. Moreover, when I enjoyed her complete beauty, why to present her a half-human? It's injustice."

Siddhartha looked at his friend with a smiling face and his head inclined towards his right shoulder, "You are a lovely person, bro! I wish she could enjoy your crazy company."

Vivek now changed the course of the discussion, "Leave my case, tell me how is Zubaan?"

"She is amazing but less than your imagination. You have changed a man into me. Your thoughts have inspired me to think about giving my services to someone, if I get a chance. Thanks bro! I love you", said Siddhartha.

"Welcome, my dear. But it is all because you are in love at present. It is easy for you to understand these feelings. In fact, I feel lucky to be a part of your love and that also is helping me heal my heart with those feelings again, as I felt about Laxmi", said Vivek thankfully.

"You know, dear. I will share all these thoughts of yours with Zubaan!"

"She will get attracted towards me then, and not towards you. fool", Vivek smiled.

"Whatever. She must know that I know a bright lover like you", said Siddhartha shaking his neck once.

Vivek laughed at Siddhartha's childish talks and said, "You are still such a boy, dear. I am sorry but I don't want anyone else to admire these thoughts of mine other than my own beloved. If you really want my happiness, do publish my thoughts, and do express them as yours. I would feel proud, if my thoughts somehow help you express your love to your beloved. If you want, I have written some poems as well. You may take them and present to her in her praise."

As Vivek was telling all this to Siddhartha, a strong urge passed through Siddhartha's mind that he was almost compelled by that urge to tell Vivek about Laxmi and tell him that his feelings will be delivered only to his beloved, but he controlled his emotions, reminding himself of the promise, he kept with Drishti, or who had taken from him.

"Hey brother, you will generate feelings in me like this. Those feelings, about which, I couldn't even imagine right now", said Siddhartha thinking in his mind—'How unlucky Laxmi is! She even doesn't want to listen about this man, and he is so mad after her still.'

"I am highly obliged, dear. I am so happy that you understand these feelings today"

"But I want to learn more, brother!"

"Sure! Your wishes are accomplished as soon as you think about them. May God bless you with all these feelings in the most dense form ever known or understood by human beings", Vivek prayed silently.

"I need your help, bro. Make me understand the smallest feeling one can feel", said Siddhartha.

"Then, listen carefully! You need to feel somebody else's feelings as your own."

"Is it? How one can do this?" asked Siddhartha.

"Let us but take your example. You love Zubaan, and also you have got a chance to work with her. Gradually, you both will understand each other. But, if at present, you express your love to her, she will be shocked for a while. What goes on with her thereafter, is what you need to know. Actually, you have to feel it. Imagine yourself as Zubaan and she as you. She approaches you and initially, you don't like her or understand her feelings, still you have to work with her. There are possibilities that you will start liking her simplicity, her patience and have compassion for her. This will weaken the walls of restriction in your heart and open them to her. And ultimately you will fall in love with her. She need not express it again to arouse those feelings in you. Even you will have questions about her liking you in your mind. Also, think that she is working normally with you after that. You will ultimately get into understanding her feelings and ask her, why she likes you? So, you understand what I just said?"

"Nothing! WOW! Kindly elaborate, sir!" said Siddhartha as if he were sleeping.

"I actually answered to your question to what if she doesn't reply! you need to wait patiently. This will help arouse feelings in her and in a pure form, if you don't repeat your proposal", Vivek finished with a cute smile.

"Oh...Okay! Now I got it. How easily you explain a thing, dear, don't you?" said Siddhartha.

Vivek stopped there for a while and smiled. "Why don't you tell her straight away that you love her and you want to marry her? That is the shortest path. How would you feel if things happen without any effort involved? You don't have anyone to praise, or find out mistakes. Isn't it what everyone is born for? Food without spices", said Vivek humbly.

"No! I didn't mean it. Hmmm...that is another way of sarcasm, you have to explain the things to me. I liked it", Siddhartha understood his friend's point about efforts in love. Waiting is one.

"Slowly patience, wait, care, understanding her nature, expressing your true feelings, compassion to calm her down when she is angry, act to make her understand those little things which irritate you, all this become your efforts, brother. God did his work in introducing her beauty to you. To carry on is something, you have to perform. You can't be mean, if you love her", said Vivek.

"And what if she is mean?"

"Your patience and care will teach her not to be mean. Time is required, I know, answered Vivek.

"Are wait, patience and time everything?" asked Siddhartha.

"No, love consists of unlimited things. There is one very important thing amongst them—destiny. If she is made for you, you will enjoy love with her and if not, you have to enjoy loving her."

"Now, is it some kind of new entry in the books of love?" asked Siddhartha again.

"It is not new. It is how well you understand destiny. Your work is to love without expectation. If your feelings are true, consistent and have the power to change the destiny, your triumph is sure. If she understands your feelings well, she will have feelings for you, which will push her as well in the same position as you do and you both will stay together in harmony. That's it", explained Vivek.

"Hmmm...I think it is good for you to think so deeply in order to keep your brain working. I need to work as well, man. I must leave now. It's already 9:45. Good night, dear". Siddhartha looked at his friend and thought—'Different, this is the word for your thoughts.'

Siddhartha was looking at Vivek, which compelled Vivek to ask him—"What happened? You were about to leave, I think."

Siddhartha looked in his eyes and smiled, "I love you, bro! Thanks!"

"What happened to you suddenly? Go home now and drive safe. It's too late now and give my respect to Zubaan tomorrow morning", Vivek understood his friend's newly developed feelings.

"Hmmm...bye", Siddhartha bid him goodbye and came out, smiled, talked to himself with confidence.'She will ask about him tomorrow. I am sure! She will'.

Siddhartha was very happy as he understood more about his friend's feelings and thoughts.

'But tomorrow it's a holiday. Despite, does it matter? I will pray for things to happen. I will cultivate feelings for my brother in her. God! Please understand my feelings as well. I can't see these feelings stay with him forever. Help me!' Siddhartha thought while driving his car.

How well managed is the system of the Almighty, how people involve themselves in somebody else's feelings and how these feelings even keep them active and involved. It was simply amazing to see a person like Siddhartha changing like that.

That night, Siddhartha slept praying for Laxmi to understand his friends' feelings. As the next morning was Sunday, he started a bit late, met his friend and his sister in the hospital and spent the evening around the nature inside a park near his apartment, only to understand the love in the surroundings. That night again, he slept thinking about Vivek, Laxmi and Drishti.

10

THE MADNESS

The next morning, he and Laxmi were working on the project. Siddhartha was still feeling sad with a little hope. He tried to complete the meeting with her quickly, as he was feeling uneasy talking to her, but unable to express his friend's feelings to her. He wanted mental peace and to think about his friend for a while to help overcome his anxiety. Hence after sometime, he said to Laxmi, "Laxmi, I think it is enough for today. You may go now and do some other work. I need to go out for some time, now."

Laxmi looked at him as he was talking without looking at her and said, "Ok sir! Thankyou for your instructions on the project. I'll work accordingly", she started moving towards the door and looked at Siddhartha again. He was at the window and there was sadness on his face.

Suddenly—

"Sir, What's his name?" asked Laxmi.

Siddhartha heard it but did not reply. These words caused a stir in his whole frame and there were but uncontrolled emotions surging up his heart now.

"Sir!" said Laxmi politely.

"Yes!" whispered Siddhartha slowly moving towards Laxmi.

"What is your friend's name?"

"What?"

"What is the name of your dear friend who loved me?"

"Vivek, his name is Vivek", said Siddhartha with tears in his eyes. He then lowered himself to hide his tears as if Laxmi understood the best of his feelings. She said, "Ok—Vivek?" and went out of the cabin.

Siddhartha took out his mobile, contacted Drishti.

"She asked his name, sis. She asked his name today!" Tears left his eyes only to increase the intensity of his feelings.

"Are you crying, bro? Don't tell me!"

Silence filled some seconds and Siddhartha said, "I don't know. But I am very happy, no words to explain on how proud I feel today to know that feelings really work."

"They do work, bro! So, what next?" asked Drishti.

"I will tell her everything about him, now. She deserves to know everything", said Siddhartha.

"You need be patient. She asked his name, so she will ask about his nature, his looks and everything as well", said Drishti politely.

However, Siddhartha was excited more than anyone else and he was still in a process to understand the power of patience.

"Won't you love to hear 'Vivek' from her mouth again before you remind her? Let her learn to ask, for she will learn more when she will ask, rather than you tell her straight away?" asked Drishti, encouraging Siddhartha to calm down his excitement and learn the way of patience to express true feelings.

"As you order, sis!" acknowledged Siddhartha.

"These are not orders, bro. It is an advice. For rest of things you are doing great. Go ahead. You are in the right direction. Learn more from your friend about feelings, as it is the time to learn from him and express it before Laxmi for the rest", said Drishti.

"Hmmm...I understand, sis", acknowledged Siddhartha again.

"Ok bro, see you in hospital. Happy for your achievement today", Drishti ended the call.

That night, when Siddhartha entered inside Vivek's ward, he was talking to sister. He greeted both of them and without disturbing them, became a part of their conversation. Vivek was sharing his feelings with sister.

"Sister! I will share my hidden treasure with you today. Don't tell anyone. I have a private account with history, where I have kept all my memories, the scenes involving me and her, her imaginations, everything with quality", Vivek said and closed his eyes.

"Clear, beautiful as ever", he said again, taking a deep breath.

"So, can you show us, one of the scenes, dear?"

"Of course. Here you are. A boy enters the classroom, where Laxmi uses to sit everyday in the school. He had noticed it during lunch on which seat she sat that day. He goes there and sits on the same seat. It is around three afternoon now and the sweeper enters into the room."

"What is he there for?"

"He has to close the room after sweeping the waste around. He asks me why I was still there. I can't share the truth with him, but still uses my emotions to make him understand and see he understands it. Everyone used to say that sweepers are rude in the school. *Naa*, they are lovely and helpful".

"But why are you sitting there?"

"Shhh...See he wants peace, as he has to breathe the same air, she breathed there during the school time. There he goes, he feels great, sitting on the same seat, where she sat that day and then closes his eyes, takes a deep breath and thinks, 'She must have breathed here today, She sat here today. Thank God for giving me a chance to come to this paradise and to feel the eternity'. He sits there until the sweeper cleans the whole room and asks him to come outside to lock the room."

"Oh My God! You really did this?" asked an astonished nurse.

"Everyday. This was my routine", Vivek smiled and opened his eyes.

"I have chills all over my body."

"Do you know sister, once it happened when I was in my engineering. It was home and was roaming around my school to revitalise the moments, I observed there in my childhood. As if, I were watching her feet, and the prints of those feet I was following very carefully. The weather was rainy. The clouds were roaring, it was lightning harder and it rained hard. As if she were still walking towards the school from the bicycle stand and I were following her feet marks on the road, which was a bit muddy. I saw that the rains were removing those imaginative marks. I immediately lay down to save the last left mark of her right feet and pasted my cheeks on it. I forgot that I was on the road and somebody would be looking at me. I was more concerned about that mark. I never wanted it to vanish like that. To save it was more important for me rather than to think about what others will think. I was still lying there with closed eyes and was feeling the rain water moving through my hair and it was still raining. Suddenly, a voice disturbed me, 'Hey what are you doing? Are you drunk? Should I help you get up?' I opened my eyes, immediately, realised the situation and replied, Oh yes, I am fine. Thanks!' I somehow managed to avoid another question from him and started moving towards my house, putting my hand on the cheeks, to prevent rains from washing away the soil from my face. I brought that soil to my house and collected it in a newspaper and kept it safe. It was pure soil, touched by her feet."

"Wait! I didn't get it. Was she really going in front of you at that time and you were following her foot prints?" asked a curious Siddhartha.

"No! as if she were there. Only he was able to see her, through his imagination", explained the sister.

"Well, that is madness and not love", said Siddhartha.

"Ha ha ha ha...Even I think so, brother. It was madness, but unconditional. I did as it was, as the thought came, without giving a second thought to reduce the effect of the passion, said Vivek.

"And where is that soil, now?" Siddhartha asked.

"At my home. Safe!" said a very happy Vivek, as if acknowledging his madness and still enjoying it, reminding himself of the place, where he kept it.

"I don't believe you, bro. I thought you were intelligent, as I have learnt a lot of things from you. I never knew, at the same time, you were mad, too. A girl can really blow a man crazy. Where is that soil in your house? I think, I should tell your sister about it. She will bring it here for you, so that you can do '*Tilak*' with it daily. You are crazy, man. What else you have treasured from that virtual girl?" said Siddhartha putting his point.

"You will understand these feelings one day, bro. You have just fallen in love. These things will happen to you as well. I really respect everything related to her, even if those were her virtual foot prints. Those are equally important for me and I put that soil behind the small temple in my house, properly wrapped in a newspaper. It's your belief that is important, not the object you believe in. But, for a practical man like you, I also have a real thing from her with me here even now?" said Vivek very politely.

"And what is that, dear?" asked Siddhartha.

"Her hair. Her real hair. And that is something very close to my heart always. Though she renounced it, but I accepted it as a gift", said Vivek very proudly.

"What? Where is it? He is crazy", said Siddhartha to sister.

"I don't know! Where is it Vivek? And where did you get it from?" asked sister.

"I told it is near my heart, sister. I was never alone. It has been always with me", answered Vivek.

"Can we see that if you don't mind?" sister was excited now.

Vivek smiled and said, "See, how excited you are to see her hair. You can imagine, how excited I have been, since the day I collected it from her desk in our school. It is inside my locket, which I have carried forever. Please take it out today. It's been around five months now I felt it in my hands. It would feel great to see it at least."

Siddhartha was watching him very carefully, and was simultaneously asking God, 'Man! Where do these thoughts come from? I mean he is just crazy!'

He came out to talk to Drishti.

"Sis, can you answer one simple question?" asked Siddhartha, grabbed Drishti's attention.

"Sure. Any time", answered Drishti and quickly moved towards Siddhartha.

"How will be these feelings transferred to Laxmi in the same form? I mean, I have no words to explain, what goes on in my self, when I see that amazing guy telling us weird things, which he had performed in love and kept safe in his heart, too."

"Actually, this is the power of reserved feelings. Love increases, if kept as a secret. Once revealed, the power breaks down, just like a battery gets discharged", explained Drishti.

"But does that mean, one should not tell one's beloved about the feelings at all?" asked Siddhartha again.

"If the person you love, acknowledges your love, surely you need do some extraordinary things to express the exact feelings. But if you don't express, surely those immature or undelivered feelings will give you joy. And when one starts enjoying himself, meaning of life is attained. I learnt this from Vivek. The way he spread happiness around is due to the pious feelings inside his heart."

"But this is contradictory with feelings of your brother. He loves her and would have loved to have her as a life partner. So, if he is enjoying alone now, why are we trying so hard to express his feelings to his beloved?" asked a burdened Siddhartha.

"I think, Vivek will answer your query better, brother. Ask him intelligently", answered Drishti.

"But how can you know what is in his mind, sis?" asked Siddhartha again.

"I know, he is a great soul and has never thought bad for someone. A good soul is always good, giving happiness to everyone in contact. It doesn't mean that we never fought with each other, but the mutual understanding is very important and I understand him. Ask this question to him about undelivered feelings and self-centricity and listen to him very carefully. His answer will clarify many doubts in your mind. But carefully, don't reveal anything to him?"

Siddhartha went to his friend's ward again.

"I was waiting for you badly. Where were you? How is Zubaan? You didn't share anything about her today. Tell me something please", Vivek said as soon as Siddhartha entered.

"I will not tell anything about her to you. Why should I tell you? What are you going to do with it? I am fed up of you man", said Siddhartha very rudely.

"I think, I have done some big mistake there. I must be punished if I hurt you. May I know the reason for this behaviour, dear?" said Vivek very politely.

"Just tell me one thing. Why are you so mean? You have kept all those feelings in your heart. Why? Doesn't Laxmi deserve to hear everything? Your story is incomplete and you want to complete my story? You want to become great....hmmm...?" replied Siddhartha coming to the point.

"No brother. Calm down first. I don't want to become great at all. I am a simple human being. Ok, let me share it with you. With God's grace, I can feel her, as if whatever is in my mind were delivered to her. My soul every day confirms to me that my feelings reach Laxmi and keep her happy", Vivek was still speaking.

"But she doesn't know anything about you", Siddhartha intervaned and suddenly realised he did a mistake.

As Vivek already had an idea that the girl Zubaan was actually Laxmi, he got a confirmation from what Siddhartha had said. This helped him to live deep and make him calmer.

"There you are. You answered the question yourself. She doesn't know anything about me means, my feelings lack the power and frequency of reaching her loud and clear. I need work more, brother. I need work more and I am always ready to do that."

Siddhartha was recording his voice in his mobile phone, in order to play it in front of Laxmi the next day.

"But that is not the answer to my query", Siddhartha raised his eyebrows.

"The answer to your query is very simple. I have some feelings in my heart for someone and I keep them there, not by choice, but as a need of time. It is not that I never tried to talk to her. I lost my control once and went to her class, as a mentor. I misused my powers of school house vice-captain. I asked the whole class to maintain strict silence and warned them of losing their internals," Vivek stopped there for a while.

"Then? Did you talk to her?" asked a curious Siddhartha.

"No. I did a big mistake there. She was not talking at all. She was actually looking out of the window quietly. Her friends were talking in fact. I called one of her classmates and asked him— 'What is the name of that girl in boy cut hairs?' However, I knew her name and straight away wrote it on the black-board, with a chalk. That was the moment; she looked at me, really much annoyed within. I understood it from her eyes, what she wanted to say. She felt awkward before the whole class. I realised it immediately and rubbed her name, but that moment made me a hopeless person in her eyes forever. It was *Diwali* celebration that day in the school, as *Diwali* holidays were starting from the next day. I tried to recover the situation though writing '*Pujan ki badhaiyan*' after the word Laxmi. But it was too late. I had hurt the beauty. I felt sorry to God and her with my soul and asked the whole class to enjoy as earlier. I said, You enjoy, I will stand outside to see if some teacher comes. Please co-operate'.

As I was standing outside really perturbed, she came out with her friend Aarti. That was the moment, she could talk to me, I presumed. But, it was her friend who asked me, 'Sir, we need to go to the wash-room please'. She avoided an eye-contact with me. I was really hurt inside and prayed God to forgive me for this silly mistake. Now, you tell me why she avoided me? Didn't she understand that I actually wrote her name? She did. This was her consciousness that she acknowledged my feelings for her, but there was a natural restriction as well. You know, why I shared this with you, dear?" said Vivek.

"I don't know really. But whatever you just elaborated, gives me an idea that she will recognise you, if someone tells her about this story. But man, I mean seriously you did that?" asked Siddhartha again.

"Yes, I did but just to fulfill my greed of talking to her or to grab her unnecessary attention. Now, I realise that I was wrong. That moment I decided that I will never disturb her like that and will love her eternally with my soul and wish for her well being always. I did not create her; she was created by nature. I had no right to disturb that beauty in the blossoms of her natural surroundings. Later that day, I went to her classroom, when the sweeper was cleaning the top floor and cried sitting at her seat, begging her pardon. And as if she said, 'It's ok, but don't repeat it'. I could feel her presence there. I opened my eyes only to find she was not there at all. I looked outside and saw her moving along with her bicycle. That was the moment to teach me, she is there with me and it is not to get her, it is to have her. That moment also gave a signal to me, that my feelings do reach her without speaking with mouth. I never wanted to hurt her like that. So, I don't know why, but I decided that I have to carry these feelings forever and increase them with the purity as a fuel. As if, I was impure or improper for her at that time and decided to pray for a positive change. I wanted to be a man without greed of anything. I thought that she must feel proud that her lover is a pious person. But don't worry, all those feelings will be kept safe as my legacy, I will leave for her to cherish. She will be proud to know that someone loved her like that. But you know, I am feeling lighter after sharing this with you today. I believe she must have forgiven me now, expressed Vivek emotionally.

"But brother, she has the right to know everything. Don't you think so?" asked Siddhartha again.

"She does and she will know everything one day. You are right. I have a secret plan for that. Don't worry. Trust me. These feelings will never go waste. God has a different plan to complete this incomplete chapter in his own way", Vivek thought about the book, sister was writing in his stead again.

Siddhartha looked at his friend amazed, as if he knew everything but didn't want to believe. He is living a half-hearted life, with all his emotions non-expressed bidding him to weep inside and hide the storm. He is an impossible guy.

"I sometimes feel too small before your purity, brother. I find myself short of words to explain what I feel after listening to your thoughts", said an amazed Siddhartha.

"And I feel so happy that in today's time, too, somebody understands my feelings and helps me assure that love exists and in its purest form. I thank God for his care given to me in the form of such a nice friend", Vivek was obliged.

Both of them laughed out loudly when Siddhartha said, "You are happy to add one more mad guy with you. Ha ha ha ha..."

The sister blessed both of them at that time, putting her hands on their heads, "God bless each of you, kind friends!"

That night, Siddhartha slept in the hospital and kept thinking about his friend. He prayed and cried in anxiety. 'Why can't I help him. I am so helpless. He is a very sweet and true person. God must help him' and he slept looking at his friend as if, God put his healing hand on his forehead.

Next day, when Siddhartha and Laxmi were working together, Laxmi saw him locking at her.

"Sir, do you want to say something?" asked Laxmi.

Siddhartha smiled. "Actually, I am trying to see that beauty inside you, which attracted my friend towards you to such an extent, that he still loves you even after seven years and that, too, unconditionally. More than anyone else I have seen him in my life, in the most amazing form. And I love him for that. You know he has dedicated his life to you and he is only very happy to be like that. And on the other hand, I see you in actual and try to ask God, why he loves you? There are questions in my mind, which you can't answer and I can't ask him. God knows, what is his destiny?"

"His destiny will be unique, sir. I really respect his feelings", said Laxmi.

"Sure", acknowledged Siddhartha.

"Would you like to listen to his thoughts, dear. I believe this will make many things clear in your mind about him", Siddhartha switched on the sound recorder.

"Sure sir", she accepted and there was complete silence after the recording was finished, as if to sow the feelings inside her for Vivek permanently.

Thereafter, they got back to work and Siddhartha was seriously working, when Laxmi asked—

"Sir, do you love him?"

"Everybody loves him. I have no doubt when I say, he taught me to love and I know how much I love him. He helped me a lot in life and changed me completely. He was there to assure me always, that I can do it. I understood the love of my parents only due to him. In short, he means love for me", answered Siddhartha very proudly.

"And why he loves me?" asked Laxmi very sweetly.

"Actually, this is what I try to figure out", Siddhartha looked at Laxmi's face again.

"But what is that he tells you, sir?"

"He says, feed a human being with feelings and don't give him anything else. He will earn everything with those feelings. On the opposite, feed a human being with everything else but feelings, he will soon destroy himself. For him, satisfaction comes from feelings. You do something for someone and he doesn't respond. You will feel neglected and this will discourage you from doing something for him in future. Still for your own feelings, you should even continue helping. About you he says that you were the one to encourage him bring himself up in life, as he wanted to make you feel the best in this world. To accomplish this, he had to be the best, so, he did everything he could, to develop himself. During this process, he achieved a lot like he became a poet, a writer, and an amazing human being I have ever met", answered Siddhartha.

“But he never approached me nor did I ever respond to him. Still he says that I changed his life. Why?” asked Laxmi curiously.

“He was always under a process to approach you, but the feelings about you give him immense in life. You gave him feelings, which satisfies his soul. You generated new synergy in him, with which he started helping people selflessly, and started a different journey altogether, where he was spreading love and in return he gets a lot more love. The source were always you. Whenever he felt a loss in energy, he used to think about you to get it. Now, you are filled up inside him to the extent the energy comes from within, as he says”, Siddhartha was explaining when Laxmi interrupted– “But how one can do it? I have never given anything to him.”

“Ha ha ha ha...I knew this will confuse you, too. But this is the reason, one should say, he is mad. But he is not. I think he is the only one, I know, who loved, did not expect and continued it. That is why everyone loves him so much. He never expects, only prays and his prayers are really bestowed, you see”.

Laxmi listened to Siddhartha and thought about what Vivek looked like.

“Sir, have I seen him ever? what does he look like?” asked Laxmi.

“Yes! Let me remind you something here. Someone wrote your name on the blackboard one day, when you were not talking. Remember?” hinted Siddhartha.

“Yes I do. But I don’t remember his face at all”, answered Laxmi.

“But why do you credit him for whatever you are today, sir?” asked Laxmi again.

"That is an interesting story itself. Five years back, I met this very simple but innovative guy. He was so eager to help everyone, which raised questions in my mind. I still remember our first meet. I asked him whether I would become famous, get good marks, wear branded clothes and silly questions like them and he said–'Yes, You will do everything. You deserve it'. I did not understand why this guy gave me the support I was looking for the whole of my life, just by saying yes to everything I was to do. Also, he sacrificed a lot for me. All our teachers used to love him, as he was an obedient student and used to respect them all. He used to request them to give me good marks in internals, whenever I got less marks and also pushed me hard to get good marks. He was so nice, you know, whenever I used to get bored, he would sing for me. He used to make different kind of things to eat, whenever I stayed with him at his. I could have never understood the meaning of a friend, if he was not there. He did everything selflessly, which encouraged me to do something for him. I started bringing lunch from my house for him, as I was a day scholar. He denied it initially, but then after several attempts from my side, he agreed and we used to eat together and this way, our bond became stronger. You know, he is a very simple human being. People used to approach him for solutions. I always used to feel proud that he is so close to me. He actually never expects anything from anyone. This is the greatest thing about him. But leave it, let us work on the project as we have very short time left."

"Just last question for today, sir. Please!"

"Ok! Ask, and you don't have to say 'please'. You have all the rights. It is just that we have to complete our work as well, dear."

"Ok sir! what does he look like?" asked Laxmi.

"What do you think, he must be looking like?" asked Siddhartha to know Laxmi's expectations.

"Well, I think, a person with such a kind heart is already so wonderful but yes, I think he must be very smart as well", Laxmi tried to imagine Vivek's face.

"Well, he is not at all smart by face but a wonderful human being to be along", Siddhartha said to check Laxmi's feelings. Though, Vivek was very smart guy otherwise.

"Hmmm...I see", said Laxmi.

"How did you see him when you have never seen, even his photograph and you don't remember his face?"

Siddhartha was thinking here, 'If his feelings really are true, then she will ask about him again. For he says– 'Feelings can do wonders'. Let me see the wonders, now."

"You know, I just try to create a picture of him in my mind, as he does of mine", said Laxmi.

This was impressive for Siddhartha, as she gave an answer to satisfy his intention, in the way, he was expecting.

"No dear, I told you a lie. He is the smartest person, I have seen and lived with", Siddhartha aroused feelings in her.

Thereafter, the whole day they concentrated on their work. Siddhartha as usual went to the hospital in evening to update Drishti and Vivek about the happenings.

"Sis, you know? I told her a lie today to check her real feelings about Vivek."

"What?" interrupted Drishti.

"She asked what Vivek looks like and I intentionally said, 'he is not smart at all, Ha ha ha ha..."

"You should never done like that. Never test the feelings, dear. It is bad", said a disappointed Drishti.

"Don't worry, I told her afterwards that I told her a lie and she happily acknowledged it", recovered Siddhartha.

"Alright, now go and meet him", said Drishti.

"I will", Siddhartha went inside to meet his friend.

"Come Siddhartha, I wanted to ask you something very important".

"Ask".

"When, where and how did it (love) actually happen to you?" Vivek asked, as if a thirsty person tried to find a well of cold water in summer.

He told him the decided that she was in his very office. As Vivek told earlier, Siddhartha had a zeal but to work, while he had the zeal to love. His point of view to see life was through love and Siddhartha's was that of work, as he was a typical workaholic. However, these days he was a very different person and was so excited about his feelings that he was thinking himself to be in a different world reflected to Vivek.

"Look at that couple. They are involved in themselves and this world can disturb them least ", Vivek pointed towards the adjacent ward.

Both of them, along with the sister kept looking there for a while and all three of them indulged into their individual thoughts.

Earlier, Vivek always used to ask himself about why we call it a 'different world?' He had got the answer immediately after understanding the chemistry between that couple. He earlier was unaware of even what he used to talk about as a normal person can't understand the kind of talks he used to do at that time—the day dreaming, the natural things like breezes and all, when others are also present there and can't feel the same environment, then something is not right. This is nothing but 'The Different World' for a person in love, with only the nature and his beloved inclusive in it. There are no blowing horns, no pollution around, no human illness, no tall buildings, no accidents, no industries, no fighting among people and nothing man-made in existence, at that time. Therefore, you are the closest to the nature when in love. You feel the winds blowing around, and see the green leaves pulsating through it. The great smell of roses, deep inside your lungs just purifies everything—your thoughts, your illness and your soul itself.

"See, how wonderful, we just felt at a mere view of this happy couple. Yeah! I forget to ask, how is everyone else around you, dear? I mean, how do you feel about your office staff, now?" asked a curious Vivek, coming back to Siddhartha.

"They have changed a lot now, they behave very well, it's happy", replied Siddhartha immediately.

Vivek smiled at him and said, "They did not change, you changed dear, which helped them understand the lovely part of you and accordingly they behave now. This is the power of love. A person's behaviour changes, as he gets into love with someone. And when Zubaan is present there, it is obvious that the atmosphere there is colourful for you."

Siddhartha could understand least out of it, still said,"That is true. Now, I understand!"

"So, where is your story nowadays?" asked Vivek again.

"Well, we have started talking to each other quite well now and we even share our problems", answered Siddhartha.

"And, do you feel that she knows about your feelings for her? See, it is a very natural thing. If she acknowledges you looking at her and signals like that", asked Vivek.

"Annn...I think so because she has noticed me many times, when I am looking at her and most of the times, she tries to ignore"..

"Beware, there is a limit of everything, that is done without permission. You should not make her feel uncomfortable. Be humble and understand her dignity. It is really important. Nobody stops you from loving her, but she should know either. You can ask her—'May I love you, you adorable' Vivek was still speaking and the sister interrupted—"You mean to say that we should ask a person, before loving him or her? How do you say so?"

"Yeah, does it make sense at all?" Siddhartha enquired.

"Let me explain at least. See. To love someone is not optional, it is natural. Ok! But the person loves you back or even allows you to love her is completely a different scenario. So, it is better ask than to create a negative image of yourself in her mind. Nobody would deny to this question. We need love. Don't we?" answered Vivek.

"That's unique thing, I just heard. Hmmm...Let us think about the repercussions of the same on others' mind", said the sister.

"There is a positive effect only, though a bit otherwise. She will either say yes or no. But the end result is an assurance that she knows about your feelings, it is smart love", explained Vivek again.

"Ha ha ha ha... You are an impossible man. Do you ever think, what you say sometimes?" said Siddhartha.

"Oh! Did I commit some mistake there? I beg your pardon, you normal human beings. I am sorry to behave as an alien. I am back as a human being, now", Vivek cracked a joke on himself there.

They all laughed and suddenly Vivek said—"You really need to love her like anything, dear. Kill expectations and rise above in the list of humble people. You get what you deserve and rest is fake. She should never feel that you are staring but your feelings should make her understand about your madness for her and she, too, must enjoy it. This is what I meant to say".

"Hmmm... I understand bro. tell me, what would have you done in such situation?" asked Siddhartha to clarify the things in Laxmi's mind.

"Listen carefully. I can understand your need to look at her with queries in mind, like why you fall, in love with her, but there are ways to do things in love and they vary from person to person. If I would have been at your place, I would have never shown it directly to her what I think about her. But, if she caught me, I would have given up myself to her completely. I would have then tried restrictions on myself. She wants the same and I try the same, what does it do? It creates a situation, where both start doing complementarily. She starts liking me look at her while I would love to see her more this way. You are getting me, aren't you?" asked Vivek.

"I tell you bro, become a spiritual leader. These kinds of things, nobody will understand and ultimately they will start believing you blindly", Siddhartha did not take it seriously.

"Ok! Leave it. I think you must follow your own ways to approach her. Don't be afraid. If you love, speak and if there is a doubt, leave it", now Vivek was straight forward.

"And what if she acknowledges my love and still things do not change between us? I mean, she still behaves as if, nothing were possible between us?"

"Now, this is what we call insecurity, bro. You haven't started yet but expectation starts. Believe in what you can do and give away. Be ready to bear ignorance and with it increase your acceptance level. I can't say, if she will change. But if you truly love her, your love will change her. Test yourself, not her!" said a confident Vivek.

"I will remember this forever, bro", said Siddhartha moving his head in surprise.

"I again tell you, her ignorance is your friend, her acceptance is your luck. Similarly, your patience is your friend and the reality is your luck. Remember!" affirmed Vivek that his knowledge must help his friend in every situation.

That night, Siddhartha kept thinking about his friend's thoughts on patience and relativity of love.

Next morning, he followed his knowledge and it helped. He straight started working on the project and Laxmi wanted to hear something else. It becomes a habit to constantly hear your thoughts from someone else. So Laxmi wanted that precious purse of feelings from Vivek through his friend Siddhartha.

"Sir, how is he doing nowadays?" asked Laxmi looking at Siddhartha's serious aptitude.

"Hmm? He is fine. See, these figures do not match", Siddhartha, concentrated on his laptop tried to bypass Laxmi's question.

"I will correct them sir, but first you tell me something about him, please. How is he and where is he?" Laxmi tried to put some pressure on Siddhartha. Laxmi started using her rights as if she were sister-in-law to Siddhartha.

"He is hospitalised and he can't move. Is it ok!" said Siddhartha without a second thought, as he was busy in the figures on the computer screen.

He was still looking at the screen even after he realised his mistake. Laxmi was just looking more at him now. He was thinking what he should say next.

"He is hospitalised?" asked Laxmi with a heavy heart.

Siddhartha looked down and at Laxmi, shook his head, breathed out, and said, "Yes, he is. Otherwise, he would have told you himself all I am telling you. It is a bitter truth that we can't change. This is also the reason, why his sister and I decided to tell you everything, before anything goes wrong".

This was really disturbing for Laxmi and she could not stay thereafter. She was an emotional girl. Siddhartha tried to stop her but she kept on saying, "This is untrue. I don't believe you at all. Why did you play with my feelings?"

"My goodness... Listen Laxmi, this is what I would have told you but only after you knew everything about him. It was not to disturb you like that. I am sorry, please. He is on his death bed at present and he would have never wished to tell you anything at this stage. But after listening to his immense feelings for you, his sister Drishti and I came to know about you, again due to his uphill feelings, we could not resist and finally decided to do this courageous task".

Tears started falling of Laxmi's eyes, and she said, "You played with my feelings. Why didn't you tell me that he is suffering so much at present? I would still have understood his feelings for me and prayed for his wellness. You are a cheater, sir. I hate you!"

This said, she went outside.

Siddhartha quickly called Drishti to tell her the worsened situation.

"Sis, that happened, which we feared of. She came to know about Vivek's deteriorating health. I am sorry, but I told her by mistake. She called me a cheater and ran out of the cabin crying."

"What are you doing here, now. At least make her comfortable. Try to make her understand. She will understand. Please, go", pressurised Drishti.

"Ok, but I think, you need to come here now and make her feel comfortable. Please, I can't handle this situation. I can't see anyone crying like that", Siddhartha got up from his chair.

"I will come there in half an hour. Handle it up to that time."

Siddhartha could not muster the courage to go and help Laxmi understand the truth. However, Drishti hurried there in less than half an hour.

"Where is she?" asked Drishti in a hurry knocking at Siddhartha's.

"I don't know. Might be in washroom. I am sorry for my mistake, sis", replied a shattered Siddhartha.

"No worries! It isn't at all a mistake, dear. It is destiny. Let me talk to her please", urged Drishti.

Siddhartha came outside and took Drishti to Laxmi's cabin. They didn't find her there. Siddhartha asked about her and they replied, "She asked for coffee and after we haven't seen her."

"Perhaps she is on terrace of the building, sis", suggested Siddhartha.

"Take me there, please", requested a more worried Drishti.

"Sure. Come."

They reached the terrace and saw Laxmi looking at the sky with tearful eyes. They neared her.

"Laxmi!" called Drishti slowly putting her hands softy on her shoulder.

Laxmi looked at her and Siddhartha. Her tear-brown eyes were breathtaking beauty for both of them. Laxmi at once understood she was Vivek's sister and hugged her tightly crying out loud to her.

"What mistake did I do that you tried to hide this truth from me?" Laxmi cried bitterly.

Drishti put her hands on her back and consoled her. "There is nothing wrong you have done here, dear. It was the time that the things were not explained to you as they should have been. We are sorry for this. You are an amazing girl. He is fine, don't worry. See, how lucky you are to have such an admirer."

"But why is he hospitalised and why did he say that his situation is deteriorating?" Laxmi dried up her tears with her hands.

"Oh! He is still a child. He might have said it out of stress. Don't worry, if you want to talk to him, we will arrange a telephone call to him in the evening for you, but do not tell him that you are Laxmi, instead you are Zubaan, as per our scheme. Promise?" Drishti gave a harsh look at Siddhartha.

"Hmm...", answered a very happy Laxmi.

"You know about him? He is a crazy man. I have heard so many different things about you from him. I don't know whether Siddhartha told you that weird truth or not. But, when in school, he used to see you during lunch, know on which seat you were sitting and after school time, he daily used to go there to sit on the same seat, to breathe the air you breathed, he says. He used to feel your presence there, after you were gone. He did say to himself, 'she must have sat here.' He took deep breaths that 'she must have breathed the same air'", Drishti smiled on her brother's true and innocent feelings.

"I know he is crazy. Siddhartha has told me many things he used to do in love with me", Laxmi acknowledged Drishti's feelings.

"He has kept one of your hair safe in his locket as well. His proud possession, you know. The four lines, he wrote on the overleaf of your photo, his personal diary, I have read. All these are the verdict of his truth", Drishti was so happy at this time that she could do anything to explain her brother's feelings to her.

"But what has happened to him? Can I meet him today, please?" asked a curious Laxmi.

"No dear, I told you. He is not in a condition you can see him. He will feel awkward, if he saw you there. It is all hidden from him, that we know his Laxmi. We have actually schemed to extract his love in the purest form, where I love a girl in my office. I tell him same crucial situations and whatever he sets thoughts over them, I share with you daily. I will give you some of his recordings as well, when he speaks but love. You surely will enjoy them", Siddhartha interrupted meanwhile.

"Oh I see, but what happened to him that he is in the hospital? And, when he will be discharged from there?" asked Laxmi again.

Before any one of them could answer, both of them got a call on their cell phones. Siddhartha got a call from Mr Amar, Bangalore to reach over there the very next day, whereas Drishti got a call from the hospital.

"Ok dear, I have got a call from the hospital. I need to buy some injections for him urgently. I will talk to you later on, in details and don't worry. Everything will be fine. Just one question before I leave from here, Do you love him?" inquired Drishti.

"I simply love his determination and the way he has carried these feelings for me, for past seven years in a row. He must be an amazing fellow to do that without getting his passion depleted. I have heard so many things, as he used to sit on my seat, breathing of the classroom air, hoarding my hair and a lot more. Now, I feel that I know him from many years. I don't know, if I love him, but I really want to be like him. Before that, I want to see him once, please", Laxmi urged again.

"Sure dear. Pray he should get well soon and then you both may enjoy ample of time together. You will receive a call from him today, but remember he will talk on Siddhartha's behalf. We planned it that way actually. You need to understand that it is for you from him straight. Ok?" Drishti brewed a very different idea.

"I need to leave for Bangalore tonight. It was Mr Amar calling to inform the same", Siddhartha informed Drishti and Laxmi about his absence next day.

"And you are Zubaan, not Laxmi. Remember!" confirmed Siddhartha with Laxmi while putting his phone in his pocket.

"Ok, I will wait for a call at least to hear him, if I can't see him at present", Laxmi got emotional.

11

THE PROPOSAL

That evening Siddhartha and Drishti decided to make Vivek ask Zubaan on phone for Siddhartha. Though it was something, Vivek would deny, they knew. Still they planned, that Drishti will insist on him to help Siddhartha somehow.

Siddhartha entered his ward first, where he found Vivek in deep thoughts.

"Hi brother, How are you?" said Siddhartha and shut the doors.

Vivek did not respond.

"Bro, listen! I need your real help today and the biggest one ever."

"Oh yes, you said something, dear? What kind of help?" Vivek turned back.

"I want you to propose Zubaan on my behalf. Feelings will be mine, words will be yours. Will you help me?" requested Siddhartha.

"No! See sister, he is asking me to propose to his beloved. What an awkward request!" said Vivek, a bit annoyed.

"Then? You only keep on telling people that they should seek help from you for their love. Now handle accordingly", sister responded.

"No", Vivek denied clearly.

He was already aware of this thing to happen, that Siddhartha and Drishti were brewing something hidden from him but for him. As if he knew, that there were no Zubaan, but his Laxmi. Even then he wanted to check Siddhartha first, to know the extent he was ready to go, to make him do this. It was not that he was playing with his feelings this way. Instead he wanted to make sure of whatsoever he might have cooked up together with Drishti, what exactly had he felt in his heart. Is it a pity only that he did for him or is it the love that Siddhartha had in his heart now which made him do it all?

"Give me at least one justification for what you are requesting me and I'll do it", challenged Vivek.

"You know already bro! I don't have the words to explain my feelings", said Siddhartha.

"If you don't have words, then wait, for they will be generated by your soul only", suggested Vivek.

"What kind of a human being he is! His ego is bigger than my love", Siddhartha deliberately disturbed his selflessness.

Vivek looked at him and said, "I am not a hard person, as you just taunted. You know that there is nothing like ego in me. Just answer to my question first."

"Why don't you understand bro? I can't live without her now", Siddhartha pleaded.

"Or at least tell me, what you feel about Zubaan. It is not that easy that you ask me and I can do it. These are your raw facts, I will share with her. I want to know, why you want her, to know everything first? What would be its outcome?"

When Vivek asked these questions, there was a complete silence in the ward, Siddhartha was now compelled to lose all his anxiety and come to the truth straight. He had to answer, as Vivek was reading his eyes at that time.

"Speak!" said Vivek , still looking into his eyes.

Here Siddhartha was thinking why Drishti was not there to rescue him.

After a few minutes, when he was still thinking, Drishti entered the ward.

"What happened?" Drishti inquired at once.

"See sis, I request him a simple thing to give his voice to my feelings and he denies for even this small help", Siddhartha tried to receive some sympathy.

"Why dear? You must help him, Come on, you can do it easily", Drishti pressurised Vivek just to do a favour to their plan.

"No! Let him answer to my questions first, sister", Vivek surveyed Drishti and Siddhartha in a sweep.

This was the moment, where Vivek knew about their plan, but still did not want to ruin the platform they had built. But, he wanted to know the exact feelings of Siddhartha in this scheme and test him as his student of love, too.

By now, Siddhartha had known, there was no escape this time. Vivek's strictness compelled him to close his eyes and pray with his heart for help from the Lord as Vivek used to do. The student had learnt to find answers for impossible questions now, through the path of prayers.

After a few moments, he knelt down on his knees in front of Vivek and said, "You made me, as I am today. It is you who taught me for these feelings, which I carry now. I am still learning to give my best in love. And I beg to you as your pupil, to teach me how to accomplish this huge task of expressing myself to Zubaan tonight? I completely depend on you to do this. Now, you as my prophet may leave me in hung or take me through this situation."

Now, Vivek could understand that Siddhartha had learnt how to pray and express the feelings with purity. Though, he might go another mile to postpone his request, but wanted to help them by participating in their decided scheme. He said to himself— "Dear friend Siddhartha, you won my heart today. Now, I can confide you to take care of my family and Laxmi, after I am gone. God bless you'.

"Now, would you help me dear?" asked Siddhartha again.

There is something in a lover that distinguishes him from the rest. It's like they know what is going to happen, as they are continuously in contact with the Lord. The same was identical with Vivek at that moment. He felt a deep thrill in his heart today, at start, he didn't know why. But now it was clear for him, too. The opportune time had come when he had to deliver the message of the Lord, the message of his love to his beloved. His wait had come to an end, now he was ready.

"Just tell me the status of your relationship? I mean, how much comfortable she is with you?"

"We are at tuned now, for she has noticed my feelings, as you suggested. Still, she will understand, without a second thought. Today, I want to tell her my exact situation, so as to make her understand the best thing that happened to me out of her love", said Siddhartha very intelligently.

"Hmmm...Please phone to her", this was what everybody wished to hear from Vivek.

"But won't she understand that I am not Siddhartha but someone else?" confirmed Vivek again.

"No, we have never interacted on phone yet. I know it is strange but true. So, don't worry, she won't recognise you", Siddhartha clarified his doubts.

"Ok, call her now and maintain silence please. Even if you feel I am cracking a joke. Dense feelings are wonders hard to understand straight. Oh God! Please help me to do my best. I need to generate some true feelings for my friend. Please forgive any false feelings from me", Vivek took a deep breath and made himself ready to speak.

Siddhartha dialed Laxmi and held the phone on Vivek's ear.

Everyone present in the ward had their heartbeat pulsate like the waves. Everybody knew that this call was being made to Laxmi, but they showed them to be ignorant of it, to maintain the dignity of the Lord's plan. The bell rang complete and none picked the phone.

"Anha... She did not pick the call", Vivek asked Siddhartha to take the phone off his ear.

"What?" said a nervous Siddhartha.

"She has your number stored, right? Otherwise, good girls don't entertain unknown numbers", said Vivek.

"Yes, she has", said Siddhartha.

"Don't worry. Let us try once more. I am sure, now she will pick the call", said a confident Vivek and Siddhartha did the same. He redialed the number and again put the phone near Vivek's ear.

"Hello!"

That divine voice, he waited for full seven years entered his ears. He thanked God for feeding him with it after a long time. He did not respond for a while. So, Laxmi asked again, "Hello! Siddhartha Sir?"

She was strong enough to hold the truth that she was actually talking to Vivek and not to Siddhartha, besides she knew she had to act as Zubaan.

"Zubaan", said Vivek, it increased the intensity of feelings inside him.

He was now waiting for the Lord, to give him the best of the words to express now, as he started speaking, while he closed his eyes and revised those moments again.

"It was a day in heaven, when I saw you. I learnt about my existence on this earth. At the same moment, a picture was formed in my mind. A picture, where I could see you as my life. I was struck hard, by the beauty that was sitting just in front of my eyes. And I had to avoid an eye contact with you, just to enjoy that moment for—I saw you. I confirmed it again just to check that I saw the real you. A strong desire went through my whole body. A desire, that was inspiring me again to try and see you. All the restrictions of the world were to be overtaken and I realised that I have started talking to God for you. I was asking Him again—'What is that you want me to do?' I just saw the face of yours and I wanted it to be mine. This I was searching for whole my life and it is you going to be there forever inside me, outside me, in my thoughts, in my deeds and everywhere. There was no doubt at all, everything was crystal clear, I had decided my destiny and was trying to seek permission from you, my Lord that may this dream become a reality soon. I don't want to give words to these feelings. No! That is not at all justified. That's something uncontrolled, a wave had passed through me and I loved to hold it inside me forever and feel the thrill incessent. I was a small kid unable to understand what exactly I had to do now and there were some constant requests sent to the God to let me know how exactly to act now. Everytime there was a question, I could see the answer as you. What do I want?– You! What am I looking at? You! What am I doing for? You! Why I exist for? You! Why do I compete? For you! Why do I love? For you! That moment clarified everything in my mind and since I have a clear vision of what I am doing, and I have been working on it.

This moment is the purest in my life. I am above any of the restrictions of the society. This is the moment when the soul is free, it's above everything and is filled with every feeling. And there is no word to express it. This is the moment when one soul is telling the truth to the other. A religion that was made for me to express your beauty to you, as seen through my eyes. To tell you why I saw you and why I understood your beauty? This is the time for all the questions to be answered and this is the time for me to follow my religion – love. The religion that was handed over to me and I cared for it for last seven years. And today I give all this to you when I ask you—will you marry me, Laxmi?"

"So, he knew it was his Laxmi and not Zubaan!" hummed Siddhartha.

Drishti understood what Siddhartha thought and placed her right hand on his shoulder, telling him to remain silent with some like gestures.

Vivek was lost, his body was here but he was in a different world. He thought his Lord to be everything.

Laxmi was listening to him spellbound. She was feeling great and happy to acknowledge the kind of lover she had. Her heart was filled with gratitude and even when she was on the phone, she was feeling shy. A strong urge passed through her heart to meet her lover at that moment. As if she wanted to listen more to him and for a long continuous period of time. She was absent from this world, as her consciousness was well attuned to his voice. There was complete silence in the atmosphere.

Everybody in the ward was so satisfied and happier to see finally the true feelings reach their destination. True love won. And she answered, "Yes, I will".

Vivek looked at Siddhartha and signalled him to take the phone off from his ears. He closed his eyes as tears blew down. He requested everyone present there to leave. He wanted to know that joy, which catelised of his eyes to flow into the floods. He could feel the weight of feelings, crystalised under the loss of seven years. He was lost and he felt himself liberated as if, he attained salvation.

Siddhartha thanked and embraced him and went out to catch a flight to Bangalore that night.

That night Vivek avoided any kind of communication with anyone, as he wanted to stay in the company of the immense happiness, of expressing. His soul was satisfied, and he affected God his 'thanks' 'You are a true magician. Indeed. Till date, I used to think that feelings are mine and I will carry them along. You proved me wrong. Even these feelings were not mine. They reached their destination and I am salvated again. I am ready for my ultimate journey towards you now. May she get eternal satisfaction and strength to live rest of her life happily and may she remember me as a yogic lover of her beauty, without any regret or dejection. I couldn't do much for her in the terms of matter but my legacy belongs to her. Please take care of her, after I am gone. Nothing was superior to love her", tears were floods, rains and uproars of his feelings. They thundered.

The next morning, Vivek was feeling very drowsy, as if nothing were in his hands. He was losing control over his eyelids as they were closing without his own wish. He called the sister.

"What's going on? I am unable to keep my eyes open!"

"Don't tell about your illness to your friend in time. Now suffer!" said the sister, a bit annoyed with his greatness.

"What is this now? Even your voice is not clear to me!" said Vivek, as his eyes got closed themselves.

"What? I am really afraid now. Let me call your sister from outside. Please take some deep breaths and remember God. I will be back soon", the sister understood Vivek's situation was getting worse. The doctor that night had told her that his body was almost ninty five per cent affected now.

Vivek realised that it was his time to leave his body to restore to his Creator and was smiling with closed eyes. As sister had gone to call Drishti from outside, Vivek rolled through whole of his life in a moment. His journey was about to conclude now. The life he lived; the love he spread; the faith he generated, all were to stay here, as his legacy. He uttered his utmost wish at such hours. He was talking to God, 'People request you for so many things, before they die. I just request you to give me that moment again, when I saw her for the very first time, as live as it could be".

He recollected those very merry moments when he moved his friend Sumer back to ask the girl to remove her knee from Sumer's and...

"Vivek, what happened? Vivek, can you hear me? Please get up for God's sake. Sister, see he is not responding. Please call the doctor", shouted helpless Drishti.

But that passionate lover had achieved what he was here for. There was no desire in life left for him. He was complete now! There were warm tears in his eyes and sweet smiles on his face. He was travelling on his ultimate journey.

On the other hand, Laxmi was working on computer in her office, when an unseen force struck her hard and she suffered from some intuition—something close was moving away from her. As though the souls were bidding the last goodbye.

She instantly called Siddhartha, in Bangalore, emergently.

"Where are you?" asked Laxmi.

"You know, in Bangalore. What happened?" answered Siddhartha.

"Take the next flight back. I want to see Vivek now, anyhow. Please sir", urged a hopeless Laxmi.

"What happened? I will come back tomorrow. Can't you wait for a day?" Siddhartha was quite unaware of the disturbances haunting Laxmi's heart.

"I don't know anything about that. I just want you. Come here and take me to him now. Please try to understand, I can't wait even a second now. I feel quite inflicted", forced Laxmi.

"Ok... ok, I am coming", said Siddhartha softly in acceptance.

"I am leaving for the airport now. I will be waiting for you the very there", Laxmi concluded.

Siddhartha called Mr Amar to tell him about the emergency, took the next flight and landed at the airport where Laxmi was waiting for her. He forgot even to make a call in the hospital, asking about Vivek.

Laxmi took Siddhartha by holding his hand; she almost dragged him into the exit. She couldn't wait for a moment. Siddhartha had already called Drishti to know about Vivek's well-being but now he was as helpless as Laxmi.

They both reached the hospital but found only the sister over there.

"Where is Vivek, sister? asked Siddhartha.

She kept mum only looking into his eyes.

"Tell me sister, for God's sake, tell me where is Vivek?" Siddhartha held sister's shoulders.

"He is no more, Siddhartha. He is no more on this beautiful planet", sister bursted into tears.

"It's impossible, sister. He can't die like this leaving all of us and all of a sudden. He has yet not met Laxmi!" Siddhartha, too, welled up of uproarous tears.

"His family received him two hours ago from here. Go! If you want to see him in the last rites, his family must have started by now."

Siddhartha was broken from inside. Just last night he was fine and talking to him and now suddenly!

"Are you Laxmi?" asked the sister by holding her hands.

"Yes, it's. I am that unlucky girl", answered forlorn Laxmi, tears rolling down from her eyes.

"God bless you dear. I could feel him in you. Now, I could understand how one could love someone constantly like him. By the way, he gave me a responsibility before dying. A book, I used to write for him at nights. The journey he travelled here along with you, but away from you. It is all in this book, his legacy, for you", said the sister remembering the great lover, who used to share everything with her.

Laxmi could not speak a word, she just accepted the book and opened the first page. Suddenly, a photograph fell down from the book and she picked it up. She could see the overleaf where it was written—

> "My definition, you complete,
> *My existence, you compete,*
> *You wrote a word (love) to say it all, on my blank sheet.*
> *I am you, you are me,*
> If I cheat you, whom do I cheat?"

Reading over these lines, she flipped the image and saw herself through his eyes, for the first time. She could feel that he has seen this photograph many times.

"Let us go, dear, for we shall be late for his last rites", intervened Siddharth, as Laxmi was in deep thoughts. The sister blessed them both from a distance, and saw off.

They hired an autorickshaw to the cremation ground. While they were travelling, Laxmi was reading the book and tears were falling off her eyes constantly. She was telling the driver to move fast.

But look! what had destiny in its store for her? They could only see, the flames, huge flames, rattling, taking him along with them into the skies! He was set free by nature. All the feelings, which got generated in him, were set free, but wait... She accepted them all as her own.

As said in *Bhagwat Geeta* by Lord Krishna– 'You didn't bring anything, you won't take anything either from here. Everything just gets transferred from one form to another.'

Similarly, Laxmi was bestowed the transfer of those purified feelings to carry them onward.

12

THE TRUE LOVE

In the end, let me take you inside a home. The home where he lived. Shhh...We are entering his room. Oh! Who is it here? Laxmi!

Why is she doing her make-up?

She is speaking to someone. To whom? Let us hear.

"I know you were here and I know you will come to see me. So, it is important for me at least to groom myself."

Now, she stands up and she lifts her hand to touch the walls in his room.

She touches the walls and says—"You must have touched these walls, these buttons. You must have seen through this window and I know, you are still here. Won't you tell today, how I am looking? Wait...What did you think? Only you had the courage to love silently?"

She becomes The Virtual Lover.

The power of true love can change a mind, the soul and everything else, a lover wants to change around him, including his beloved.

13

POEMS

He articulated some poems for everyone, while his stay in the hospital.

For My sister Drishti

Distances are made with the crack in Ice (patience),

Then nothing matters about who is nice (you lose the lovely people too),

The words they become hard to hear,

As they don't come out, out of fear,

The only way to hear is to see,

If there is an eye with a tear!

The terms of life are not so easy,

They make us hard, also busy,

No rain, no pain, no gain in such time.

I am still strong, want to fight,

My revenge will surely bring light,

My patience is the strongest hit,

With it, in any situation I befit!

Let the problems come in the way,

I'll not cry and still say,

I'll neither stop nor dry,

As I'll always try, as I'll always try!

For My friend Siddhartha

Though I'll leave you someday but will always be there,

You can bring joys and sorrows to me, to share,

I'll always love to see you happily married,

Would love to cherish the moments we carried,

A great friend were you to me, I'll always miss,

I have told my wishes for you to my sis,

I pray God to bring happiness in your life,

May overcome you each strife.

Don't forget your parents too, who gave their all,

They worked hard to make you strong and tall,

Don't hurt anyone and let others also enjoy,

Please keep my thoughts alive and take care, Boy!

For My beloved Laxmi

I love you is my mistake, everyone told me!

I couldn't tell you, myself hold me!

You are not away if in my Heart;

My feelings are pure not a dirt;

Your friends are not few but a list;

I am a poor guy, look like mist;

A great girl and a great friend;

You wear anything and make it a trend;

You are so nice, hard to loose;

Get you, then nothing to choose;

I know how much I feel;

But know that myself to deal;

The situation is so deep;

I feel sometimes to weep;

Why are you so far being so near?

Why my thoughts to you, are not clear!

And... One day in my life, my dear I get.

When my eyes are not wet;

I feel your hug; I smile for a while,

We walk together, involved, for a mile.

My breaths you take again, with the way you look at me.

"Do that again", would be my plea.

On the grass, again you hold my hand and ask me to sit.

I try to reduce the distance, by coming closer a bit.

You understand my feeling and smile and hide.

The moment compels me to be loyal and abide.

Oh my dear, let it be again!

Come closer, let me forget my pain.

Lets together again, we shine!

Please be mine, please be mine!

Again, we dip inside the ocean of love,

Again, from the restrictions we rise above,

Again, you find me the most amazing,

Again, you look at me and keep gazing,

Again, in my arms, you hold me from behind,

Again, you become the only thing in my mind,

The words you whisper in my ear and say,

You love me by soul, not the body of clay,

I again rest my head on your shoulder with blind trust,

The purity of my feelings clears all- the dust and the lust,

Give me a chance to rise before this world and say again,

I lost my everything, for you as my gain, for you as my gain!

For My Critics

I will go, someone else will come,

The people admiring me will be some,

I did something good, one would say,

It will make my critics mum;

I'll go in a matter of days from your thoughts,

My deeds will be remembered only in fear of droughts,

I'll still pray that you all live with Love and respect,

If some problem occurs, blame me; let me be the suspect,

I'll feel lucky that I was the bad, and out,

Give bad words to me, in anger, you shout,

You all will be Happy and I'll be satisfied,

This is the thing, for which I lived and cried,

This was my dream, for which I was so stubborn,

I pinched your teeth like the dried corn,

I was a worm you all kept telling me,

I did not shy, so you kept selling me (Making fun of me in Public),

I am gone and leave you on your own,

Laugh on me now loudly come' on,

Just a little love I wanted though,

Another person dies and go,

Live happily and forget me now,

Don't even remember about, I was how!!